"You
too

"Tell me something I don't know, Kirrily," Ryan replied.

"I'm no longer a naive sixteen-year-old. You have to stop regarding me as some kind of bimbo who's going to fall into the arms of the first smooth-talking male who comes on to her."

"I don't wish to encroach on your love life, but I do have strict rules about you bringing men home."

"Oh, goody, *more* rules! And they are...?"

ALISON KELLY, a self-confessed sports junkie, plays netball, volleyball and touch football, and lives in Australia's Hunter Valley. She has three children and the type of husband women tell their daughters doesn't exist in real life! He's not only a better cook than Alison, but he also isn't afraid of vacuum cleaners, washing machines or supermarkets. Which is just as well, otherwise this book would have been written by a starving woman in a pigsty!

Alison Kelly has a warm, witty writing style you'll love! Bubbly heroines, gorgeous laid-back heroes...romances brimming over with sex appeal!

Look out this month for **Boots in the Bedroom!** by Alison Kelly in THE AUSTRALIANS.

Books by Alison Kelly

HARLEQUIN PRESENTS®
1903—YESTERDAY'S BRIDE
1975—MAN ABOUT THE HOUSE

Don't miss any of our special offers. Write to us at the following address for information on our newest releases.

Harlequin Reader Service
U.S.: 3010 Walden Ave., P.O. Box 1325, Buffalo, NY 14269
Canadian: P.O. Box 609, Fort Erie, Ont. L2A 5X3

ALISON KELLY

Ryan's Rules

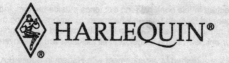

HARLEQUIN®

TORONTO • NEW YORK • LONDON
AMSTERDAM • PARIS • SYDNEY • HAMBURG
STOCKHOLM • ATHENS • TOKYO • MILAN • MADRID
PRAGUE • WARSAW • BUDAPEST • AUCKLAND

ISBN 0-373-18699-1

RYAN'S RULES

First North American Publication 1999.

Copyright © 1996 by Alison Kelly.

This edition published by arrangement with Harlequin Books S.A.

Printed in U.S.A.

PROLOGUE

'GOT a minute?'

The sound of his sister's voice drew Ryan's concentration from the quote he'd been working on all afternoon, while the sight of the two steaming mugs she carried drew his smile.

'Kid, if you've got coffee, I've got more than a minute!' He accepted the cup from her hand. 'Thanks. This Emmerson project looks like being an even bigger pain in the rear than I expected.'

'You'll cope, Ryan. You always do.'

'Coffee *and* flattery! You've not only got my attention but my curiosity too. What's up—a delinquent account causing you problems?'

'Er, no. No, everything is fine in that department, which is why I've decided to fly over and join Mum and Dad in Europe.'

Shock removed Ryan's ability to swallow the mouthful of coffee he'd just taken until the need to question his hearing forced him to gulp it down; he opened and closed his mouth twice before he could even *think* of a response, let alone voice one. Had Jayne announced she could walk on water, he wouldn't have been half as stunned.

'You're doing *what*?'

'You heard me,' she said, looking as if she wasn't sure she could repeat the words. 'I'm thirty-four years old, Ryan; it's time I got my life together.' She smiled.

'At least, that's what everybody's been telling me and…well, I decided yesterday they were right.'

On one level Ryan wanted to cheer with joy. On another the suddenness of his sister's decision worried him. Ever since the death of his best friend, Steven, Jayne's fiancé, fifteen years ago, he'd wondered if she'd ever put the past behind her; until this minute there'd been no noticeable indication that it would happen. Apprehensive about the suddenness of the decision, he searched her face for an answer.

'Don't look at me as if I'm having another breakdown, Ryan.'

'I wasn't!' Yet despite his denial the possibility *had* drifted through his consciousness. Trying to smile away his guilt, he rounded the desk to take his sister's hand. It was soft, fragile and surprisingly naked.

'You've taken your ring off.' His observation drew a weak, shiny-eyed smile.

'Last night. I think that was the hardest part. Flying to Europe is the easy stage.'

The admission was made in little more than a whisper, but the subdued strength behind the words swamped Ryan with a mixture of love and relief so great that it was easier to wrap his arms around her and draw her close rather than speak. Finally, after more than a dozen years, his little sister was ready to push free from the shadows which had cocooned her; her mourning was over. When he finally held her away they were both smiling.

'Have you told Mum and Dad?' he asked.

'Yeah, I rang them before I came into work.' She laughed. 'They were stunned, thrilled and relieved, in that order!'

'I'll bet.' He hesitated before adding, 'And the Cosgroves?'

Jack and Claire Cosgrove were their folks' best

friends and currently touring Europe with them. They were also Steven's parents.

'They were pleased too...' There was a slight break in her voice. 'Claire said Steven would've been glad to know I was getting on with the business of living.'

Ryan nodded, then immediately steered the conversation back to lighter topics. 'Well, from what Mum said when I spoke with her the other night you'll *love* Italy! So—' he leaned across his paper-scattered desk and retrieved his coffee '—when do you fly out?'

'Sunday.'

'*Sunday!* But today's Friday. What about a passport and visa—?'

'They're up to date. Remember, I nearly did this a couple of years back?'

He remembered. K.C. Cosgrove, Steven's younger sister, had all but convinced Jayne to take a vacation with her, but at the last minute Jayne had backed out and nothing anyone had said had been able to change her mind. If nothing else, perhaps the very impulsiveness of this decision would prevent Jayne from having second thoughts this time.

'OK. Then I'll ring Mrs Phillips right away and organise for her to come in and cover for you in Accounts and—'

'Mrs Phillips isn't available, but it's OK,' Jayne assured him. 'I've arranged for Kirrily to cover for me.'

'You can't *mean* that!' Even as he said the words Ryan knew the worst. 'Aw, Jayne! *Please* tell me you didn't ask K.C..'

'It's all arranged; she's arriving tonight.'

'Then *unarrange* it or *I'll* be courting a nervous breakdown.'

'Oh, stop it, Ryan!' she chided him. 'It's the perfect solution. Kirrily's currently out of work—'

'She's a *soap actress*, not an accountant!'

'I'm not an accountant either. Besides, she did two years at business college.'

'K.C. did *two* years because she flunked out the first! What's more, she's only a kid—'

A chuckle interrupted him. 'If you still think of her as a kid you obviously missed the episode of *Hot Heaven* where she was practically nude and—'

'Spare me the run-down on that soap opera,' he said drily; his body was reacting to the scene he unfortunately *hadn't* missed.

'Ryan, what's the problem? It's only for a few weeks.'

He grunted. 'Earthquakes occur in mere seconds.'

'I should've guessed you'd be difficult about this.'

'Jayne, honey, I'm not trying to be difficult. I'm trying to be *practical*. As much as K.C. is like one of the family, asking her to do this isn't a good idea.'

'Why?'

'*Why?*' he echoed, feeling as if he'd been hit from behind by fate in a ten-ton truck. 'Because...well, because she's so damned *flighty*. Heck, a person never knows what she's going to do from one second to the next! And she *hates* being told what to do. *Especially by me*,' he added ruefully. 'Hell, she'll question every decision I make. Plus her face is so well known that she'll have every person who walks into the place wanting her autograph or trying to hit on her. How much work do you think she'll manage to get done?'

'Look, Ryan, this trip is important to me, but I'll cancel if—'

'What? Uh-uh...no way!' The thought that he might provide Jayne with an excuse to back out of her plans overrode the instinct to preserve his sanity. 'Put that idea right out of your head! You're going. You'll be on that plane Sunday and K.C. will be sitting at your desk first thing Monday.' Glancing down at the quote which had been giving him so many headaches, he sighed. Compared with living and working with K.C. for the next few weeks, everything else was going to seem like a picnic!

As a kid K.C. Cosgrove had always had a knack for throwing him off balance, one minute tugging at his heartstrings and making him putty in her hands and the next grinding away at his patience until *his* hands had wanted to tighten around her cute little neck. Then, during her rebellious teen years, she'd done her best to develop her ability to manipulate Ryan into an art form, which had caused numerous heated debates between the two of them. But what bothered him the most was that now, at the ripe old age of twenty-four, K.C. had unexpectedly acquired yet another unsettling trait—the ability to send his thirty-six-year-old hormones into a frenzy.

CHAPTER ONE

KIRRILY spied his tall frame waiting by the luggage carousel at first glance. Even if his black jeans and leather bomber jacket hadn't contrasted with the business suits of late, Friday-night commuters, Ryan Talbot would have stood out in a crowd. Six feet six of solid male athleticism and rugged blond good looks weren't easily overlooked—at least, not by any red-blooded woman with a pulse.

Unfortunately, Kirrily was forced to concede that not only was she red-blooded but *her* pulse was positively *rabid*! Anxious to gain some control over its excited thumping, she stopped dead in her tracks and took a deep breath. Aside from its causing several fellow passengers to cannon into her, nothing happened. Great!

Up until Bob and Pam Talbot's fortieth wedding anniversary a few months back, she'd been convinced she'd outgrown the teenage crush she'd had on their son, but now, at the age of twenty-four, she'd relapsed into a severe bout of the hots for one Ryan Talbot! As if she didn't have enough problems!

She sighed. After what she'd left behind in Melbourne, being in Sydney was a godsend, even if it meant exposure to Ryan.

An impatient shove and a frosty look from a well-groomed matron reminded her she was impeding people's progress. Muttering an apology, she again started moving towards the waiting Ryan, wishing she could quash the tingle of adrenaline which increased with each step she took. It wasn't fair! A grown woman wasn't supposed to react like this to a man who still saw her in pigtails and braces. Realising the male in question had now spotted her, she fixed a serene smile on her face, determined not to let him rile her. She was an adult; she could control both her tongue and her temper. And this time while she was around Ryan she would control them simultaneously! Even if it *killed* her! No matter *what* he said!

'G'day, short stuff!'

The term would have been an insult even if she hadn't been five feet six, but her vow of self-control and maturity demanded that Kirrily wait until he actually did pat her on the head before she hit him! No pat was forthcoming. Instead Ryan bowed from his superior height and brushed his usual kiss across her cheek before stepping back and studying her from head to toe. Though irritated under his detailed, blue-eyed scrutiny, she forced herself to relax—at least as much as it was possible for her to relax around Ryan; it seemed these days whenever they got within sight of each other the air around them thickened to a point where she could almost chew it.

His inscrutable expression made her wish that she could think of something witty to say. Heck, she'd settle for something inane, if only for the reassurance of knowing she was still capable of thinking of *anything* besides how damn good Ryan looked! Good? Ha! The guy was as sexy as sin!

'So how was the trip?'

It took a second for Kirrily's hormone-corrupted brain to register the question, but, grateful for the nudge back to reality, she rallied quickly.

'Lousy. We took off from Melbourne in a storm and it stayed with us most of the way. Still, it was worth it to escape another Melbourne winter.' Not to mention everything else, she added silently.

'I didn't know you were a baseball fan.'

Her confusion was caused as much by the question as the effect of his dazzling grin.

'Your cap, kiddo,' he said, coming dangerously close to having his orthodontically correct teeth knocked in as he patted her on the head. 'By the way, you put it on backwards. Now, tell me which bags are yours and let's get out of here.'

'I didn't ''put it on backwards''. I'm wearing it backwards *intentionally*! And for your information it's a basketball one.'

He raised a surprised eyebrow. 'Your bag?'

'No, my cap!' she snapped, yanking it from her head and holding it so that the Sydney Kings insignia was visible.

'Good to see living in Melbourne hasn't swayed your home-town loyalties. Now, if you'll rein in that temper I see flashing in your eyes,' he said, 'and tell me which bags are—'

Spying her two pieces of luggage, she reached to grab them but missed when another commuter pushed past her. Only Ryan's steadying hand prevented her from ending up spread-eagled on the carousel and vanishing from sight as her luggage now was.

'K.C., I said to tell me which was yours, not try and crash-tackle the thing yourself.'

The amusement in his tone didn't do much to lessen her irritation and embarrassment. She refused to look at him as they waited for the bags to reappear.

'Next time they come around,' he said tersely, 'just *point* at them. I want to get out of here before you're recognised and we've every starry-eyed soap fan in the place stampeding for an autograph.'

'Ryan, this is Sydney, not Hollywood; I'm hardly going to cause a stampede. Besides, I'm sure you'd protect me to your dying breath—whether I wanted you to or not!'

'Don't bet on it,' he said drily. 'Now, quit acting like a spoilt brat and tell me which bags are—'

'That one and that one!' she snapped, annoyed that *he* had no difficulty in snaring them as they came past. 'And don't blame me if I live down to your low expectations!'

He frowned. 'What's *that* supposed to mean?'

'It means that maybe if you stopped treating me like a petulant child I'd stop acting like one!'

'Well, that's one thing we agree on,' he said.

'Alleluia! We agree I'm an adult!'

'No.' He smirked. 'We agree you're petulant.'

K.C.'s expression, before she pivoted and hurried towards the exit, told Ryan that if she'd brought her trademark sense of humour with her from Melbourne it was packed in the bottom of one of the two suitcases he held. Great! K.C. riled up was the last thing he needed.

Had time travel existed, Ryan would have booked a trip back to the day when K.C. had gone from being cute to sexy and stopped it happening. But of course there was no such thing as time travel and, what was more, he couldn't pinpoint the transformation of Kirrily Claire to any set event.

He suspected that the evolution had been a gradual thing, and it was only irritation at finding himself physically attracted to her which caused him to feel as if she'd actually catapulted from one to the other. Still, it seemed as if one minute he'd been chaperoning her sixteenth birthday party, dressing her down for spiking the punch, and the next he'd been at his parents' fortieth wedding anniversary, mentally undressing her! Not that the clingy creation she'd worn that night had left much to a man's imagination! Even the tight jeans and polo-necked bodysuit she wore now were an improvement on *that*, though they, too, hugged her subtle young curves to the point of distraction!

Her pursed-lip silence continued all the way to the car and Ryan felt like a heel—not because he'd upset her but because he'd welcomed the opportunity simply to look at her without having to listen to her. Prize bastard that he was, he'd even gone so far as to walk *behind* her just so that he could study her cute, denim-clad butt! The fact that he'd found himself speculating on what it might look like minus the denim almost choked him with guilt.

She was his late friend's *kid sister*, and he knew Steven Cosgrove hadn't meant this when he'd made his dying request that Ryan 'keep an eye on little K.C.'! Hell, if Steve had been alive today to witness Ryan lusting after his sister, he'd have knocked his so-called best mate's teeth down his throat. And fair enough too, Ryan reasoned; *he* wouldn't tolerate anyone leering at Jayne the way he had at K.C.!

Get a grip, mate! he told himself. She's not your type at all. You like 'em blonde, buxom and classically beautiful, not brunette and boyish with pixie-cute smiles and basketball caps—even if their legs do stretch into tomorrow!

But the way his feelings kept flipping from platonic caring to physical attraction worried the daylights out of Ryan. In the past he'd reasoned that much of the protectiveness and tenderness he felt for K.C. was accounted for by their families' close bonds and the fact that he was twelve years older than she. So why was it that all of a sudden the gap between thirty-six and twenty-four seemed narrower than the one between sixteen and twenty-eight? It wasn't—

'Don't tell me you've locked the keys inside?'

K.C.'s impatient tone dragged him from his troubled thoughts; automatically he checked his pockets. 'No.'

'So why are you standing there scowling at the car? Trying to *terrify* the doors into opening? Hurry up, will you?' she urged. 'I'm dying to talk to Jayne.'

'You'll have plenty of time. She's not flying out until Sunday.'

'That's if she doesn't change her mind.'

'You think she will?'

She shrugged. 'It wouldn't be the first time.'

Kirrily forced herself to slide into the the passenger seat of his car without commenting, but she had to bite her tongue, *hard*, to maintain her assumed indifference. Ryan's passion for Jags was no secret and over the years he'd restored more than a few. Now apparently he didn't need to satisfy himself with second-hand ones; this beauty was the latest in the XJ series and Kirrily knew that it wore a six-figure price tag. The look on Ryan's face told her he was waiting for her traditional request to be allowed a test drive, so he could give *his* traditional answer—*no*. Perversely she bit down even harder. Besting Ryan, even in such a small matter, was worth permanent teeth marks in her tongue!

Kirrily managed to keep stubbornly silent until Ryan had steered the sleek vehicle into the evening traffic, then she shifted in her seat, smugly satisfied by the puzzled frown marring his forehead. *Gotcha!* she thought gleefully before speaking.

'This decision of Jayne's was awfully sudden,' she said. 'The first I knew of it was last night.'

'The first *I* knew of it was a couple of hours ago.'

'You're kidding. She didn't sound you out on the idea first?'

'Nope. Just walked into my office this afternoon, told me she was going and you were covering for her at work.'

The response startled her. Ryan was every bit as pedantic about protecting Jayne as he was Kirrily, but while she'd started bucking 'Ryan's Rules', as she tagged them, at sixteen Jayne's fragile emotional state had made her more compliant to her brother's wishes. In fact Kirrily had never known her to make a big decision without 'running it by Ryan' first.

'Have you spoken to Jack and Claire?' he asked, without taking his eyes from the road.

'Yeah, last night. I phoned them straight after Jayne called.' She smiled. 'They're thrilled, of course—like your folks.'

'Mmm.' The glance he tossed her was too quick to read. 'And what about you, K.C.?' he asked. 'Are you thrilled?'

'Well, sure!' she said. 'Of course I am. Who wouldn't be? It's about time Jayne started to do normal stuff. Not that I think she *hasn't* been normal!' she amended hastily, knowing how Ryan tended to be sensitive about references to Jayne's past emotional problems. 'Just *withdrawn*. But...well, she's only thirty-four and an attractive woman. And—' She broke off in the face of the cynical look Ryan gave her.

'Don't try and kid me, K.C.; we both know Jayne's existence has been more than ''withdrawn''. It's been positively ritualistic.'

'I'll admit it's been routine—'

'Stop soft-peddling round the facts,' he muttered. 'She's spent the last fifteen years like a mouse on a treadmill: going through the motions of life without living it! Now this comes from right out of the blue.' He thumped the steering wheel. 'Wham! Six weeks ago, she was commemorating Steve's death with her annual pilgrimage to Kiama and today she announces she's flying to Europe.' He shook his head. 'Believe me, much as I'd like to be able to relax and feel good about her breaking out of her rut, the truth is, I can't.'

Having braked at a red light, he looked across at her, the rhythmic flashing of a nearby neon sign alternately highlighting and disguising the concern in his face. What had started out as an angry outburst ended in weariness. 'You're as uncomfortable about this as I am. So don't sit there telling me what you *think* I want to hear.'

'I'm not,' she insisted. 'I'm really thrilled she's decided to…to get her act together. Everyone's been praying she'd do it for years and now, finally, it's happened. It's a good thing and we—' She stopped under his disbelieving glare.

'Oh, OK! OK!' She sighed. 'I admit a *tiny* part of me is worried because, like you said, this came from out of the blue. But there's a difference between *saying* you're going to do something and actually *doing* it. You're worried Jayne hasn't thought things through; I'm worried she might start, that she'll begin wondering if she's acted too hastily and back out.'

His frown prompted her to add, 'A person who makes up their mind quickly can change it just as fast. If Jayne senses we have doubts about her decision, she'll have doubts. So I think it's important we don't reinforce the negatives in this. The bottom line is that she needs to do this; why she's decided to shouldn't be an issue.'

There were a few seconds of silence as Ryan obviously mulled over what she'd said, then he turned a bemused smile in her direction.

'You know, K.C., you surprise me at times. That's a very astute observation.'

The praise had been too patronisingly bestowed for her to accept it graciously. 'Well, you know what they say—out of the mouths of children…'

His grin did things to her insides that she both loved and hated. 'Actually it's out of the mouths of *babes.*'

'I know.' She gave him a sickly sweet smile. 'But I hate being called a babe. Besides, I'm trying to wean you off the image of me with a teething ring.'

'You could try wearing a muzzle,' he suggested. 'You'd not only present an alternative image but I'd stop worrying that you were going to bite my head off every time you misconstrued an innocent remark.'

'You know, Ryan, this will probably be beyond the realms of your imagination…but there are some men who find the idea of me sinking my teeth into them *very* appealing!'

A wave of nostalgia swept through K.C. as the car swung into the driveway of the house which had been so much her second home in her teenage years that when people had asked for her phone number she'd given them the Talbots' as well. However, in the five years since Ryan had bought the house from his parents, when, like hers, they'd retired to Victoria, she'd made only a handful of visits and never stayed more than a few hours. For the next three weeks at least, this would be where she was staying.

'What's up?'

She smiled in response to Ryan's curious stare. 'Nothing. I was just thinking how everything looks exactly as I remember. I always expected you to do some kind of renovations.'

'Why?' He frowned. 'What's wrong with the house?'

'Well, nothing! It's…it's just that I'd expect, you having been an architect and having access to building equipment at cost, you'd be tempted to make changes.' She smiled. 'I mean, I *love* the little house I've bought, but boy, if I had the money I'd *really* do something with it! You, however, *do* have the money.'

He raised an eyebrow.

'Oh, stop looking like that,' she chided him. 'All I ever hear from Mum is how incredibly successful you are and how you've quadrupled the company's profits since taking over from your father.'

'Claire exaggerates,' he said.

'Claimed he, sitting behind the wheel of the latest-model Jaguar,' she responded drily.

He grinned. 'I didn't think you'd noticed.'

'Not a chance!' She laughed, letting her fingers caress the dashboard and no longer bothering to hide her appreciation of the vehicle. 'So…do I get to drive her while I'm here?'

'Like you said...not a chance. I've seen you drive, K.C.'

'Huh! You're the one who taught me.'

'Don't remind me. Jayne said you can use her car while she's away.'

The reference to his sister caused her to glance across to the house. 'You know, Ryan, maybe now that Jayne's finally putting Steven's death behind her it'll let the rest of us do the same.' She looked back at the man who had been her late brother's best friend and almost his brother-in-law.

His gaze narrowed. 'Meaning?'

'Meaning maybe now someone will tell me *all* the facts surrounding the night he was killed.'

'K.C.—'

'No,' she said, raising a hand to stop his words. 'I know the things that happened *after* he was killed: about Jayne's phantom pregnancy and her subsequent break-down. I even think the real reason you've never let me drive one of your cars is because Steve was driving yours when he was killed.'

He tensed noticeably at her words and reached for the doorhandle. 'Don't go formulating a lot of half-baked ideas about something that happened when you were nine. Let it go, K.C. It looks like Jayne finally has.'

'Have you?'

It wasn't until he wrenched open the driver's door and activated the car's interior light that his irritation was visible.

'I don't know what kind of fantasies exist in that over-imaginative mind of yours, but keep them to yourself! I don't want Jayne upset.'

'Is that the reason why, when your parents wanted to sell this house and Jayne didn't want to move, you bought it?' Without answering, Ryan got out of the car and slammed the door shut. 'I'm right, aren't I?' she persisted as she, too, climbed from the car. 'That's why you haven't done any alterations to it, because you didn't want to do anything that might upset Jayne.'

His jaw tightened as if he was clenching his teeth. 'I thought out-of-work actors waited tables and drove taxis. I had no idea they dabbled in psychoanalysis.'

'You know me,' she said, shrugging. 'I'll try anything once. As a matter of fact I'm looking forward to doing the accounts for Talbot's.'

Moving to the open boot, he grunted, 'That makes one of us.'

'Ryan?' she said, coming around to lean against the boot of the car as he removed her luggage. 'There's one thing I've never been able to understand…'

'How to quit while you're ahead?' he suggested.

'Why you gave up a partnership in one of Sydney's most prestigious architectural firms to take over running a building-supply business? I mean, all you ever wanted to be was an architect; you graduated top of your class from university—'

'Well, of course you don't understand *that*, K.C.!' He slammed the boot closed. 'The reason is based in responsibility—*family* responsibility! Our fathers and Steven worked damned hard to build up the business and I for one had no intention of watching their efforts ruined at the hands of outsiders out to make a quick buck.'

'So you don't miss architecture?'

'At the moment all I'm missing is the peace and quiet that existed before I picked you up at the airport. Now, will you just shut up and let me get these bags inside so I can go hunt up the Prozac I got last time you were here?'

CHAPTER TWO

ON SUNDAY Kirrily was again at Mascot airport; this time, though, she was in the International terminal watching Jayne's plane roll down the runway. Fighting to keep her emotions in check, and unsure how much longer rapid blinking would continue to keep tears at bay, she slipped her sunglasses from the top of her head down onto her nose. The action drew the attention of Ryan, standing beside her.

'You want to go?' he asked.

'No...not unless you do.'

The hope that he'd missed the slight tremor in her voice evaporated as he deftly removed her sunglasses.

He swore. 'Aw, you poor kid. Don't cry.'

She jerked away from the touch of his hand on her shoulder and lifted her chin. 'I'm not crying!' she insisted as two huge tears rolled down her cheeks. 'Nor am I a kid.'

'Fine. But in that case I think you should know your eyes are melting.'

She tried hard to muster some anger towards him—she really did—but the wealth of understanding and gentleness shining in his eyes negated her efforts. This was one of those times when kindness was the hardest thing to take.

'Damn it,' she muttered, a sob rising in her throat. 'I...I had no intention of crying. It's stupid. I...I...'

Kirrily wasn't sure which she surrendered to first, the flood of her tears or Ryan's strong, comforting embrace, but it was a relief to give in to both. It was as if the warmth of his body and the sensation of his hands stroking her head and back were releasing all the emotions she'd kept penned up for months. Crying felt good. It mightn't be constructive, but it felt good!

'Shh, honey,' he whispered. 'Jayne's going to be fine. It's not as if she'll be on her own; the folks will be there for her.'

Though she nodded against Ryan's chest, Kirrily knew she was reacting to more than just the significance of Jayne's leaving. With the stress she'd been under in recent weeks and the disappointment of leaving the cast of *Hot Heaven* she'd been a prime candidate for a serious bout of waterworks.

She considered telling him about the turmoil she'd been going through during the past few months, but thought better of it. The last thing she wanted to invite was a dose of Ryan Talbot's brotherly sympathy, which was as suffocating as his over-protectiveness; better to let him think her tears revolved entirely around Jayne's departure.

She drew a deep breath with the intention of trying to stop the half-sobs still raking her body, but instead of regulating her respiration it made her dizzy. Not the light-headed dizziness which preceded fainting, but the fuzzy, blurry, *aroused* kind, caused by inhaling the earthly masculine scent that was uniquely Ryan. She shivered as a shower of electric sparks erupted in her bloodstream. Crazy as it was, she couldn't stop herself from nuzzling closer. Just a few seconds longer then she'd step away from him…

Ryan knew he had a problem the moment K.C.'s arms locked around his waist, but when she went limp in his arms and shivered a part of him told him he was in *deep* trouble. And unfortunately his brain hadn't been the source of his intuition.

Placing his hands on her hips, he gently eased her

away from the lower half of his body. The last thing he wanted to do was embarrass her.

'Er...K.C...?' he said hesitantly. 'Are...are you all right?' Her face remained pressed into his chest, but there was a slight nodding movement of her head. 'You're sure?' he urged, hoping that the more inane he kept the conversation, the quicker his body would settle down. But, given its slow rate of recovery at present, Ryan figured he'd have to start reciting nursery rhymes pretty soon. Another attempt to withdraw further from her had her arms tightening. He sighed, torn between the need to comfort the distraught woman in his arms and the need to save what little dignity he had left; God knew, his self-respect was right out the window!

Comfort the distraught woman? K.C. wasn't a *woman*! Yeah, right, mate! his brain chided. So how come you're in such bad shape, then, huh?

OK, so technically and physically Kirrily *was* a woman, he rationalised, but she was also Steve's kid sister! Why the hell was he having such a hard time remembering that lately? Why, after more than two decades of thinking of her in a wholesome, brotherly way, was he suddenly being plagued by constant speculation of what it would be like to make love to her—the kind of hot, heavy love which left both participants hungry for more of the same?

I'm sick! he thought with disgust. I'm really, really sick!

'Yeah, you do look a bit pale.'

Ryan groaned when Kirrily's observation made him realise he'd spoken his thoughts aloud. Yet as he looked into her frowning, concerned face he couldn't help smiling. Even with red-rimmed eyes and her face mottled the tell-tale pink of a crying jag Kirrily Claire Cosgrove was beautiful; he took a perverse sort of comfort in knowing that there was no way he'd be the only man to make a fool of himself because of her.

A suspicious light came into her green eyes. 'What are you grinning at?'

'Nothing I want to talk about. What say we head to the bar?'

She knew her face reflected confusion, but she couldn't help it; Ryan usually pushed the teetotaller ideal at her. 'The *bar*?'

'You look like you could use a drink and I *know* I need one.'

'I thought you felt sick.'

'It's mental not physical,' he said, taking her arm and steering her towards the lifts as she shot him an impish smile.

'Oh, that's OK, then! For a minute there I thought it was something unusual.'

Schooling his face into a look of disappointment, Ryan shook his head. 'Too predictable to be witty, K.C. I've come to expect better from you.'

'I'm sorry. I keep forgetting that, unlike yours, the precedents *I've* set are of an exceptional standard.'

'Better!' he praised her, a slow grin spreading across his face. 'A load of absolute rubbish, but that, too, is typical of your standard!'

Despite the elbow she jabbed in his ribs, Kirrily smiled, glad to discover they were back to their familiar banter-and-bicker relationship. It was, she'd decided, the safest way of dealing with her recent feelings towards Ryan. Though the short time spent in his arms had been wonderful, knowing that from his perspective it was purely platonic was murder on her feminine pride. Not being into masochism, Kirrily resolved to cure herself of this latest bout of 'Ryan fever' before she ended up making an idiot of herself.

When they reached the bar Ryan steered Kirrily to a corner table and pulled out a chair for her.

'Scotch straight up, isn't it?' he queried.

'Er, yeah... Thanks,' she said, feeling incredulous

when he merely nodded and went to place the order. At his parents' anniversary he'd been openly disapproving of her drinking spirits, not because he rarely drank anything except the occasional light beer but because he'd assumed she was drunk. And he'd started verbally tearing strips off her without giving her a chance to explain that the reason she'd been stumbling her way around the dance floor had been that Aidan had been so damn full that he'd barely been able to stand, much less dance as he'd insisted! But by the time Ryan had finished admonishing her Kirrily had been too angry with both men to care about offering a defence.

She sighed. While there had been times in her teens when Ryan had been justified in thinking the worst of her, she wished he'd stop judging her on her prior record. Irritated to realise she'd been staring at him ever since he left the table, she redirected her attention to her surroundings.

The bar, designed in a relaxed, open-lounge style, wasn't crowded. Laughter rang out from one table occupied by a group of foreign flight attendants. At another what was obviously a family group seemed to be passing the time before an awaited arrival or departure and at the far end of the room two couples chatted in animated whispers.

It struck Kirrily that this was the first time she and Ryan had socialised together as adults without either their parents or Jayne being present. In the years since she'd attained the age of eighteen they'd only interacted at family functions and traditional celebrations such as Easter and Christmas.

The friendship between the Cosgroves and Talbots stretched back to the childhoods of Kirrily and Ryan's fathers; they'd grown up next door to each other, married local girls and then proceeded to raise their children within a few blocks of each other. Later it had been friendship rather than economic sense which had prompted Kirrily's father to inject funds into Bob Talbot's financially strapped business when the banks wouldn't; thus a personal relationship had expanded into a professional one.

Ryan slid into the seat opposite, interrupting her thoughts.

'Here you go,' he said, putting his orange juice on the small, low table separating their chairs and placing her drink in her hand. 'Scotch straight up; no ice, no water, and, I promise...' he smiled, sheepishly '...no lectures.'

His subtle reference to the incident at his parents' party caused Kirrily's stomach to flip. Then again, the cause might have been the sensation of feeling his fingers close over hers.

'Don't tell me you can read my mind now?' she asked, the idea scaring the hell out of her.

'God, I hope not!' He looked aghast. 'What you *do* gives me enough headaches, let alone knowing what you *think* about doing!'

'Your headaches are self-inflicted. No one's asked you to keep sticking your nose into my life.'

'Your big brother did.'

The blandness of his response didn't disguise the emotion in his eyes and Kirrily lowered her lashes as her mind flashed to the memory of Ryan walking into Steven's room after the funeral and discovering her sobbing her nine-year-old heart out. She remembered how he'd sat down on the floor next to her and quietly started to tell her that he missed Steven too, that he'd loved her brother every bit as much as she did and that maybe it would be better if they were sad together. It was then that he'd said she was to think of *him* as her brother now, because Steven had asked him to take care of her for him.

'And Jayne, too?' she'd asked.

'Yes, Jayne too,' he'd said. 'We'll both have to take care of Jayne, K.C..'

That was the first time he'd called her K.C.; until then no one but Steven had ever called her that. Now only Ryan did.

Kirrily stared into her drink and sighed. Strange how Jayne's decision to get on with her future had made everyone else so much more sensitive to the past... It was the first time in years that Ryan had made reference to her brother's dying request.

Ryan changed his mind and began wishing he *was* able to tap into K.C.'s thoughts!

The lines marring her brow bothered him, nearly as much as his urge to reach out and stroke them away. In the past he'd taken pains to avoid mentioning Steve in front of K.C., never again wanting to see her hurting as she had been the night of the funeral, when he'd found her crying, curled up in the corner of Steven's bedroom clutching his football jersey, all alone. It had ripped his heart out, and with hindsight he'd often wondered if Steve hadn't somehow foreseen that his little sister would be almost overlooked in the emotional turmoil that had enveloped the adult members of both families. It was cruelly ironic that when Jayne had taken the final step in letting go of the past he'd been the one to toss it carelessly in the face of an already distressed K.C.

But had it really been done carelessly?

Ryan's gut churned at the unbidden question, but before he could examine where it had sprung from K.C.'s voice distracted him.

'What?' he said, trying to refocus his mind. 'Sorry, I missed what you said.'

'I know.' She smiled and lifted her glass. 'I suggested we drink a toast to Jayne. I think it's kind of appropriate, don't you?'

'Very,' he agreed, raising his glass. 'To Jayne. May this be the start of a happier life.'

She touched her glass to his. 'And may I remember everything she told me about the Talbots' accounts.'

And she added cheekily, 'I'm *certain* you'll drink to that, Ryan.'

'K.C., I won't only drink to it,' he said, 'I'll *pray* for it.'

The way she sipped her drink then let the tip of her tongue creep across her lips as she savoured the Scotch caused Ryan's stomach to clench. Desperate to douse the fire erupting there, he tossed his juice back in one swallow.

'You know, Ryan...'

He told himself that her smile wasn't intended to be sensual. Nor was the way she hooked a long strand of dark hair behind her ear and exposed the soft young skin of her jaw and neck to him.

'I might surprise you,' she continued. 'But knowing you *expect* me to stuff up will stop me from feeling guilty if I do.'

Ryan merely grunted. She wouldn't feel guilt because right now *he* held the monopoly on it!

When they returned from the airport Ryan dropped Kirrily at the house then went to the office to catch up on some work. He wasn't back by the time she took herself off to bed at the puritanical hour of eight o'clock and he was gone when she arrived in the kitchen, showered and dressed, at seven-ten on Monday morning.

Which was a good thing, Kirrily decided, picking up the kettle, because even on her best days no one had ever accused her of being a morning person, and after the sleepless night she'd endured she wasn't in the mood for a bright-eyed, bushy-tailed and invariably dry-witted Ryan Talbot. She did, unfortunately, find evidence of his regrettable existence in a note shoved under a magnet on the refrigerator.

Expect you on the dot of nine and not a minute later!

Try not to dress theatrically—i.e. NO BASKETBALL CAPS! If Jayne's car needs petrol go to the garage at the intersection—I've a company account there.

   PS—I've already fed Major. But don't forget to activate the house alarm.

Kirrily screwed up the note and hurled it across the room, her actions sending Jayne's usually sedate Persian rocketing from the kitchen in a blur of blue fur.

'Why, you arrogant, patronising, smart-alec jerk!' Unable to satisfy her pre-caffeine rage with a civil vocabulary, she resorted to a stream of expletives and another shout of frustration. He seemed to delight in treating her like an imbecile!

'No basketball caps'! Huh! It was bad enough that he considered her brainless, but for *him* to have the audacity to question her dress sense as well! *He* whom his mother had practically had to sedate to get him into a dinner jacket so he could escort Kirrily to her debutantes' ball! *He* who considered ties as something one put on a garbage bag so stray dogs couldn't rummage through it!

Why was it that all her life Ryan had felt it necessary to dish out advice to her, to vet her boyfriends, to watch over her like some sort of guardian angel? What did he think she had parents for? A mental picture of her mother asking, 'Well, what does Ryan think about all this?' popped into her head and she swore again.

That particular image was only a couple of months old, the comment coming when she'd told her parents that she was donating her acting services to a condom commercial in the interests of safe sex. Kirrily, of course, hadn't discussed the matter with Ryan, but remaining silent hadn't protected her from his opinion. Recalling his terse phone call to her after the commercial had been screened was enough to make her cringe...

'K.C., don't you make enough on that soap you do without broadcasting your sleeping habits to all and sundry?'

'I didn't get *paid* for doing it,' she'd hastened to explain. 'Well, except for the hundred free samples the company sent me!'

Unlike her, Ryan hadn't seen the funny side of that. She just wished she could have seen his face when the courier had delivered the fifty condoms she'd sent him! She'd included a note stating that she doubted she'd get through all one hundred by the use-by date so she was generously splitting her profits with him! Visualising Ryan's reaction to *that* was amusing enough to dampen her anger.

Trying to be objective, she looked at what she was wearing. OK, so her black ankle-length skirt and boots were this winter's latest fashion, but surely even the most conservative of dressers wouldn't find them theatrical? And as for the polo-necked bodysuit she'd teamed them with... Well, admittedly it was a vibrant red, but she intended wearing a black blazer, so she needed a bright contrast to stop her from looking too severe.

'Stop it, Kirrily!' she ordered. She knew she was more than acceptably attired for work in an office, but as usual Ryan's habit of expecting the worst from her had caused her momentarily to question her own judgement. She really hated it when she did that—hated *him* for having such influence over her! A desire for retaliation tempted her to march back to her room and don the shortest, skimpiest dress she'd brought with her! Thinking of the emerald Lycra number hanging in her wardrobe, she giggled.

'Now, *that*, Major,' she said as the cat waddled back into the room, 'has what I'd call an Academy-award shock rating.' The animal turned its squashed-in face towards her and miaowed. 'You're right,' she said, proceeding to organise some breakfast for herself. 'Much too obvious a response. Not to mention childish. I'm staying as I am. But boy,' she vowed, 'am I going to rattle his cage when he least expects it!

*   *   *

'Kirrily, this is Ron Flemming. He's our senior sales rep and my second in charge. Ron—Kirrily Cosgrove, Jack's daughter; she's covering for Jayne while she's away.'

As Ryan introduced her to the last of Talbot's Building Supplies' thirteen full-time employees Kirrily smiled and extended her hand.

'My wife and kids aren't going to believe me when I tell them the star of *Hot Heaven* is working with me,' Ron said, a friendly smile and a slight flush spreading over his chubby thirty-something face.

'Thanks for the compliment,' Kirrily said, 'but I wasn't the star.'

'You were as far as my mates are concerned!' Ron countered. ''Specially after the episode with you and what's-his-name in the bath.'

Kirrily rolled her eyes at Ron's teasingly lecherous grin. 'I don't think I'm ever going to live that down! People are *still* asking me if I was really nude or wearing cover in strategic places.'

'Were you?'

'*Ron*,' Ryan interrupted, 'aren't you due out at the Perrelli site?'

'Yeah, but not for—'

'Then I suggest you get out there.'

Sympathetic to anyone on the receiving end of one of Ryan's glares, Kirrily produced her brightest smile. 'We'll have heaps of time to talk, Ron. I'll be working here for at least three weeks.'

'The operative word being *working*,' Ryan muttered, guiding her away from the salesman's desk. 'I'm not running a Kirrily Cosgrove fan club here.'

'I'm sure there's some union rule which stipulates employees must be allowed to talk to each other in their lunch hours,' she retorted.

'I wouldn't know. I'm not up on union rules; round here *I* make the rules, and number one is, Don't go flirting with my male employees! Especially the married ones.'

Kirrily was genuinely shocked. Oh, sure, the general public tended to perceive the acting fraternity as being morally corrupt, but in reality she'd not found actors any worse or better than people outside the industry. That someone who'd known her as long as Ryan had would make such a comment, even light-heartedly, irked her.

'For your information, *Mr Morality*, I would *never* hit on a married man!'

His mouth twitched. 'Good. Then we won't have a problem with rule number one, will we?'

'No, but, knowing you, there are probably another hundred or so I'm expected to keep.'

'Hard to say,' he said, looking pensive. 'It's an open-ended sort of thing. But don't worry—as they occur to me I'll give them the next sequential number and pass them on to you.'

'Gee, thanks! You know it was lucky for Moses that it was God and not *you* handing out the commandments, otherwise he'd still be carting them down the mountain.'

'I know,' Ryan said, holding open the door of Jayne's office and motioning her through. 'God and I considered that at the time.'

Annoyed because she couldn't keep her face straight, she punched his arm as she walked past him into what would be her office for the next month.

The first thing she noticed was that the desk, which had earlier been clear except for a telephone, blotter and calculator, now had three stacks of paper on it, one of which was a very large stack. At a glance she identified it as invoices and statements; the other two were letters and promotional catalogues. Obviously Julie, the firm's receptionist, had distributed the mail while Ryan had been introducing her around. Now it was time for Kirrily to 'get down and dirty', so to speak.

'Look, when you feel like you're getting snowed under just let me know, OK?'

Ryan's words jerked her head back up. He must have picked up on the hint of apprehension she was feeling, but he hadn't said, *if* you feel you're getting snowed under... Oh, no! He'd said *when* because, as usual, Ryan thought she didn't know what she was doing! And he— big, kind-hearted white knight—was rushing to rescue her without even waiting to see if she needed, much less *wanted* rescuing!

'Listen, Ryan!' she said hotly. 'I can handle things!'

'I know but—'

'Jayne spent all Saturday explaining things to me and, contrary to what *you* expect, *she* was convinced I could cover this job without getting "snowed under".'

For a moment she thought he was going to argue the point; instead he shook his head as if he were taking the biggest risk of his business life by just letting her into the building. Reaching for the typed list of duties that Jayne had left for reference, she studied it as if he wasn't there.

'I take it, then, you don't have any questions you want me to answer?'

She racked her brain for one he wouldn't be able to answer.

'Well, then, K.C.,' he said, and started from the room, 'I'll leave you to it.'

'Wait! I do have *one* question.' She produced an innocent smile.

'Yes?' he prompted, glancing at his watch as if calculating whether there was time to give her an answer in three one-syllable words or less. He frowned at her continued silence. 'Well, what is it you want to know?'

'How are you off for condoms, Ryan?' Fighting to keep her face bland, she looked him right in the eye. 'Be sure and let me know if you need any more.'

Apart from a minuscule tightening of his mouth, there

was nothing to suggest she'd fazed him. His silky smile revealed even white teeth and superiority. 'Thank you, K.C., but I'm well covered in that area—pardon the pun. I bought a new box last week.'

'A *new box!*' Kirrily felt her jaw practically hit the floor! 'You've used *fifty* in *two* months?'

His ocean-blue eyes widened a fraction as if he himself was surprised by the fact, then he shrugged. 'Who counts?'

Obviously she'd been under a misconception—she flinched at her own pun; she'd assumed that since busting up with the gold-digging peroxide blonde who'd adorned his arm last Christmas Ryan had been burying himself in his work. Apparently that wasn't all he was burying himself in! *Fifty* in less than *two* months—what did that average out at? Mentally she couldn't begin to work it out, but surely most people would be bedridden with RSI doing it that often? And she'd called him Mr Morality! Ha! More like Mr Amorality.

'Now, K.C., if there's nothing else…'

Mutely she shook her head.

'In that case we can both get on with our work, then.'

The minute he was out of the door, Kirrily reached for both calculator and desk calendar. Fifty in two months?

CHAPTER THREE

FOR Kirrily the first few days on a new project always passed quickly. She found the excitement of working with new people and the challenge of a new task pleasantly invigorating on a mental level. However, the first few days of working for Ryan passed *too* quickly! It seemed as if the eight hours a day she should have had to perform her duties had somehow shrunk, and by five o'clock on Thursday she was forced to concede that she was further behind with the accounts than she wanted to be and light years behind where she should be. Though she'd been as busy as a workaholic bee all week, there was no evidence of it, and when Ryan found out it wouldn't be honey-sweet praise he'd heap on her!

Rats! Where had she gone wrong? She'd followed the instructions that Jayne had left to the letter, being careful to maintain the other woman's rigid routine. Careful? She'd been downright pedantic!

The daily duties were simple enough: attach any incoming account statements to the appropriate invoices from the previous month, check the pricing of incoming invoices against the original quotes then input them into the appropriate creditors' records on the computer. Jayne had said that the task could take anything from a few minutes in the middle of the month to three or four hours at the start or end of a month. With a glance at the mountain of paperwork sitting on her desk, Kirrily dropped her head into her hands.

'Oh, no,' she groaned, not even wanting to think about

how far behind she might be by the end of the month.
Already she could practically hear Ryan verbally tearing
strips off her for her ineptitude. Unfortunately she could
also hear the sound of the locks on the front entrance
being thrown, which meant that any minute now he-
who-was-her-boss would saunter into her office and tell
her it was time to call it a day. Not that he practised
what he preached.

Considering the hours Ryan put in, he must have set
himself the goal of becoming a millionaire before the
year was out. Who was she kidding? If he'd worked like
this for the last five years he already had to be a *bil-
lionaire*. No wonder her parents marvelled at the divi-
dends they received! He was gone from the house each
morning when Kirrily got up and, so far, every night this
week he'd not come back until after eleven.

After his remarks about the condoms, she'd thought
that perhaps he was spending his time with a woman,
until her cat-killing curiosity had led her to find the condoms she'd sent him, still in sealed boxes, in the upstairs
bathroom cabinet. That she'd been flooded with relief at
the discovery bothered her as much as his absence all
week! Either he was a workaholic or he was avoiding
her. Call me paranoid, she thought sourly, but I'd lay
bets it's the latter.

It wasn't that she expected him to entertain her, but,
after sharing her house in Melbourne with two friends,
she was used to having someone with whom to exchange
news of the events of the day. Spending the last four
nights alone with only Jayne's overfed, over-pampered
Persian for company hadn't been her idea of a good
time; Major might be a willing listener, but his conversation left a lot to be desired.

'K.C.!'

At the sound of Ryan's voice, she grabbed ninety per
cent of the unprocessed invoices and shoved them into

a drawer, barely managing to shut it before his shadow fell across her desk.

'Time to pack it in, K.C.. It's gone five.'

She looked up, hoping her guilt wasn't showing, and feigned a grimace. 'Has it? Darn! I've still got a few invoices to get through,' she said, motioning towards the half-dozen accounts still lying on her desk. 'Sorry. I guess the day got away from me.'

'No doubt while you were catching up on old times with Trevor Nichols,' he said, his disapproval evident.

'Look, they shouldn't take me too long to get through,' she said. 'I'm sure I can have them done in no time.'

'Really?' Ocean-blue eyes regarded her with scepticism. 'What did he come in for?'

She blinked. 'Who?'

'Nichols.'

'Oh. He wanted to know what he owed on his account.'

'And how much was that?'

She scrambled to think. 'Uh, less than two hundred dollars, I think.' She pulled the computer keyboard closer. 'I can call up the details for you—'

'No need. Did he pay it?'

'Well, no, but he's coming in tomorrow.' Ryan looked far from pleased. Obviously the Nichols account was a dodgy one. 'If you're worried I could put a "stopped credit" notation on his file—'

'Don't bother. I don't have the slightest doubt he's good for the money *or* that he'll be back in tomorrow.' His intent gaze, which moved from her by now less than neat French braid all the way to her skirt, which had ridden up way past what was businesslike, caused Kirrily's stomach to flip-flop. Quickly she swivelled her chair around so that the desk could shield her legs and averted her eyes.

'Um…well, I might as well get on with finishing these

invoices,' she said, wishing that her voice didn't sound as if she was suffering the early stages of laryngitis. Swallowing hard, she reached for the offending papers. 'Like I said, they won't take me long.'

The intercepting touch of his hand on hers was so unexpected that for an instant she thought she'd been electrocuted; given the way her heart and lungs momentarily ceased functioning, it wasn't an unreasonable conclusion. Looking up, she encountered incredible blue eyes; her heart went from still to turbocharged in nothing flat.

The heat rising through her body had nothing to do with guilt or embarrassment and everything to do with the fact that she was a normal, healthy woman and Ryan Talbot was sexy enough to reactivate the pulse in a dead one. She'd have liked to think that she didn't appear half as rattled as she was, but common sense voted it a faint hope.

Then in a blink he was leaning nonchalantly against the filing cabinet, causing her to think that she'd only imagined his thumb caressing her wrist.

'Leave them,' he said, his voice gravelly. 'A few invoices are hardly worth the bother of you staying late.'

Knowing there were about fifty more than a few, Kirrily cursed his generosity. Staying late was her only hope of catching up. 'It's no bother; I've got nothing planned tonight.'

'Forget it!' He straightened with the same abruptness as he'd spoken, then grimaced and massaged his neck. 'I'm not leaving you here alone.'

'Alone?' she echoed. 'Aren't *you* working late?'

'Yeah,' he said, 'but I'm ducking down the pub for a counter meal, then coming back.'

'Oh.' She smiled as the solution came to her. 'Then I'll go have dinner with you first and—'

'No!' With an expression of absolute dread he abandoned his neck massage to rake at his already much

fingered hair. 'K.C., I'm meeting with a local builder
and plumber to discuss a project; it's business. The last
thing I need is you distracting them from it.'

'Well, gee, Ryan, if you're *that* worried I'll burst into
a song-and-dance routine in the middle of your sales
pitch on downpipes and cistern cocks, I could always sit
at another table.'

A smile tugged at his mouth as he gave her body a
very male once-over. 'No way,' he said. 'If I walked
into that pub with you there'd be more sales pitches
flying on cistern cocks and downpipes than a nice girl
ought to hear.'

'And what's *that* supposed to mean?'

He shook his head. 'Nothing! Here—' he shoved her
handbag and jacket at her '—be a good girl and go
home. OK?'

'Fine! I'll go home!' Though his condescending tone
made her angry enough to want to storm off in her best
Thespian huff, she didn't want to run the risk of his
finding the hidden invoices should he need to get anything from her drawer. 'Do you mind if I at least tidy
up a little and turn off my computer first?'

'By all means do whatever is necessary.' He strode to
the door. 'But *hurry*; my meeting's scheduled to start in
ten minutes.'

Yeah, right! And my execution is scheduled for tomorrow, she thought miserably. There was no way she'd
get that invoicing done now. Although perhaps if she
came in early and skipped lunch…

'Oh, and K.C.—' about to open the drawer where
she'd stuffed the invoices she froze '—do me a favour
and feed that damn cat before you go to bed. If there's
not a constant supply of food in its dish the animal gets
nasty. He attacked me the minute I walked in the door
last night.'

Desperately regretting the fact that Major wasn't a

killer Dobermann, Kirrily nodded. 'Sure,' she mumbled. 'No problem. Feeding the cat will be the high point of my evening.'

'Damn stupid lock...' Kirrily grumbled as her key failed for the second time to find its destination in the near-darkness.

Any other night the house was lit up as if Ryan had shares in the electricity company; tonight it was darker than London during the Blitz. It was already somewhere between three and four in the morning and at this rate she'd be lucky if she got to bed before the sun rose! Had she taken Jodie up on the offer of the sofa she could have avoided the fight with the front door. Dead tired, all she wanted to do was fall into her bed and sleep for a minimum of twelve hours, but even knowing that she was only a few hours away from having to appear perky and professional at work wasn't enough to make her regret her impulsive decision not to spend another night at home. She mightn't be the proverbial party animal, but she wasn't a recluse either.

Finally the key found its mark and she waved a dismissing hand to the cab driver who'd solicitously watched her progress down the driveway to ensure that she wasn't mugged before getting into the house. A few months ago she'd have laughed off as ridiculous the possibility of that happening to her, but not any more. An involuntary shiver shook her body and she determinedly willed her mind back to the matter in hand.

Mindful of Major's habit of trying to escape at every opportunity, she eased the door open just wide enough to squeeze through then quickly pivoted, shutting it a second before she felt the cat dart past her leg. 'Sorry, Major,' she whispered into the darkness. 'I win again.'

Sportingly the cat curled around her shins in welcome, but as Kirrily leaned down to pet it a hand closed around her upper arm. Her heart stopped mid-beat, raw terror paralysing her and choking her hysterical scream to a mere whimper.

'Where in God's name have you been?'

Enmeshed in fear as she was, not even immediate recognition of Ryan's voice calmed her. Though her brain told her she was safe, her body hadn't accepted the fact; her heart continued to pound in her ears and her skin still crawled with goose-bumps.

It's Ryan, her brain chanted. It was only Ryan who grabbed you. Ryan won't hurt you.

'Answer me, K.C.! Do you have any idea what time it is?'

No matter how angry he sounds, Ryan wouldn't ever hurt you. It's OK. You're safe—

Light suddenly flooded the entrance hall, its intrusive glare making her close her eyes. She sagged back against the wall, grateful to have something other than her trembling legs to support her.

'Geez!' Ryan's voice dripped with disgust. 'You're so drunk you can barely stand up!'

Kirrily knew she should have been furious, with both the accusation and the delivery of it, but the relief and fatigue monopolising her body left little room for indignation. She was safe. Nothing was going to happen to her. As the realisation sank in it was impossible to suppress a smile.

'This isn't a laughing matter, K.C.!'

Slowly she rolled her head against the wall. 'I'm not drunk, Ryan,' she said wearily. 'A tad tipsy, a little tired and in severe shock, but definitely not drunk.'

'Good! In that case you'll at least be able to open your eyes and explain where the devil you've been all night and why you didn't see fit to let me know you were going out!'

That was when Kirrily discovered that even in shock she had a very short temper. Oh, she opened her eyes all right! And she saw red! The parentally outraged tone of Ryan's words had been bad enough, but that he had the audacity to look as if he actually expected her to answer him was simply too, *too* much!

'I...beg...your...pardon,' she enunciated, through gritted teeth, 'but you are *not* my father! Nor am I accountable to you for my comings and goings.' She refused to be intimidated by his narrow-eyed glare. 'I might be working for you, Ryan Talbot, but I clock off at five and what I do after that is *my* business and nobody else's!'

'Like hell! It's mine while you're living under my roof, damn it! Do you have any idea how worried I was when I got home after midnight and you weren't here?'

'I'll bet not half as worried as I was when I walked in the door a few minutes ago and got mugged in the dark!'

'I didn't mug—'

'You scared the living *stuffing* out of me!' she raged, holding her hand out in front of her. 'You think I shake like this for no reason?'

The sight of her small, delicate hand trembling in midair between them and the tears streaming down her face made Ryan want to cut his throat.

Hell! She wasn't angry, she was damned near hysterical! Consoling her became his first priority, and once it did drawing her into his arms became as automatic to Ryan as his next breath. Expecting her to fight him but instead having her fall willingly against him and wrap her arms around him as if she feared to let go worried him far more than her earlier absence had.

K.C. didn't like him coddling her—he'd known that for years—so what the devil had happened to her tonight? Knowing she was too distressed for him to question, he instead tried to calm her.

'I'm sorry, honey,' he whispered. 'I didn't mean to scare you.' Keeping his voice soothingly soft and low, he stroked her head in the gentle, repetitive way he'd used to calm Jayne over the years. 'It's just that I was waiting for you and when I heard a noise at the door I came straight on through; I never thought about turning on the lights. I'm sorry. Shh, take it easy. It's OK.'

He had no idea how long he stood propped against the wall with her fragile frame leaning into him; it seemed like mere minutes, yet at some point he must have dozed off because the next thing he knew with any real certainty was that K.C. had fallen asleep and the hesitant light of dawn coloured the room. Stiff from having one leg braced against the wall for balance, he shifted slightly, trying not to disturb K.C., whose head rested against his chest.

The serenity she reflected in sleep was so at odds with the energy she emitted when awake that Ryan was helpless to stop himself from tracing the arch of her right eyebrow. While K.C.'s features were too elfin to be called classically beautiful, what otherwise might have been called prettiness was enhanced by her gypsy-like colouring, which hinted at mystery and passion. Ryan watched as his palm moved to caress her amber-tinted cheeks; they were softer than anything he'd ever felt.

When she innocently turned her face deeper into his touch, he cursed both his quickening pulse and his morals, wondering how feelings of pure tenderness could so quickly transform themselves into lust. Had he possessed these feelings with any other woman, nothing would have stopped him from swinging her into his arms, carrying her upstairs and tossing her into his bed. But this was K.C., so once again he mustered a nobility and resolve that must surely have qualified him for sainthood and lifted her gently into his arms.

Holding his breath as she snuggled closer, he carried her towards her own room, steadfastly determined to ignore the heat coursing through his body and the images burning in his mind.

* * *

Kirrily threw back the covers and glared at the digital clock which, despite what the mid-morning sunlight flooding her bedroom was telling her, was showing the time as 6:07 a.m.; her wrist-watch, however, confirmed her worse fears—it was nearly *eleven*!

Ryan wasn't just going to kill her, he was going to submit her to the slowest torture imaginable!

Shedding herself of the clothes she'd worn out the night before, she tried to recall exactly what she'd done after collapsing like a hysterical idiot all over Ryan. She couldn't remember unplugging the radio alarm, but obviously she had.

'Great!' she muttered, shoving her arms into her robe and pulling the waist cord tight enough to rupture several internal organs. 'As if he isn't going to be ticked off enough because the invoicing isn't up to date!'

For a split second she debated which she needed first—a shower or a cup of coffee. She hurried to the kitchen; showering while the coffee perked would save time.

'God, how could I have been so stupid?' she roared. 'I'm beginning to think it's some sort of genetic thing...'

Ryan!

She stopped dead as her feet hit the cold slate of the kitchen floor. 'Wh...what are *you* doing here?'

He wiggled the mug he held. 'Drinking coffee. You want one?'

She wasn't sure if her initial reaction to seeing him sitting at the table was shock or horror, but in the face of his calmness confusion was paramount. It *was* Friday, wasn't it? Surely she hadn't slept for over twenty-four hours? No, of course she hadn't! So why wasn't he at the office? Forget *that*! Why wasn't he asking why *she* wasn't at the office, *demanding* an explanation for her tardiness? Heck, maybe it *was* Saturday!

Ryan watched the parade of emotions across K.C.'s

face, wondering how she could manage to look both childishly bemused and sexy at the same time. Then he decided that the plunging neckline of her robe and the way it parted as she moved hesitantly towards him was a contributing factor to the sexy part. As was her sleep-tousled hair and the way she gnawed at her bottom lip.

'Is today Friday?' she asked.

'Yep. All day.' Grinning at her confused expression, he held his coffee-mug towards her. 'Since you're up, you want to pour me another?'

'*What?*'

'Sorry. Could I get you to pour me another cup of coffee, *please* K.C.?' She blinked then shook her head as if to clear it. 'On second thoughts,' Ryan said, getting to his feet, 'it'll be quicker if *I* get the coffee.'

'OK, Ryan, you win,' she said.

He turned back to see her propped against the refrigerator, her arms folded. 'Win what?'

'If this isn't *The Twilight Zone*, how come you're asking for coffee and not explanations as to why I'm not at work?'

'Because I know why you're not at work. Want me to pour you one?'

'I *want* you to explain why you aren't frothing at the mouth and telling me how irresponsible I am.'

'For what?'

'For sleeping in!'

'You only slept in because I turned off your alarm. It's hardly your fault.'

She crossed the room in a flash and, heedless of the mug he held, grabbed his shoulder. '*You* unplugged my clock?'

'Hey, watch the coff—'

'Forget the coffee and look at me!'

He obliged. It was no hardship looking into her wide, dark-lashed green eyes first thing in the morning, even when they were flashing fury and bore evidence of slightly smudged mascara. All in all the effect was disturbingly sexy.

'Why, for God's sake?'

'Because you were exhausted and needed the sleep.'

'Damn you, Ryan! I'm not a child. I can decide for myself if I need sleep or not; I don't need your help! I've survived on less than three hours' sleep before and not collapsed from physical exhaustion!'

Her face was flushed with anger and frustration, but he'd anticipated no less a reaction from her. Kirrily prided herself on being self-reliant and resented unsolicited help from anyone. She resented *his* help so completely that she *never* bothered to solicit it; others did so from time to time on her behalf, but since Ryan never revealed as much it was he whom she perceived to be interfering. So be it, he thought; this time her behaviour demanded his intervention whether she liked it or not!

'It wasn't your physical exhaustion which concerned me, K.C.,' he said, matching her glare with one of his own. 'You were an emotional *mess* when you got home this morning.' He paused only long enough for his words to sink in. 'I want to know why.'

'*Why? Why?*' she echoed in a way that made him suspect that she was searching for a plausible reason rather than the truthful one.

'I'll tell you *why*! Because you—' she jabbed his chest '—jumped me in the dark and scared ten years off my life!'

'Not good enough,' he said. 'That wasn't a normal reaction to mild fright, K.C.; you were close to freaking out completely. Something else happened last night so don't bother to deny it.'

She looked as if that was exactly what she was going to do, then her shoulders slumped as she drew in a deep, resigned breath.

'OK, if it'll make you happy, I'll give you a blow-by-blow account of the night. Satisfied?'

'I'll let you know when I hear it.'

'I was lonely, so I phoned around and arranged to have dinner and a few drinks with some of the guys at the club. There are *some* people,' she said pointedly, 'who aren't embarrassed to be seen out with me!'

'*What* guys?' He knew that more than a few of K.C.'s old boyfriends still had the same one-track minds they'd had as teenagers.

She rolled her eyes. '*Girl* guys. Megan Tang, Crissie Webber and Jodie Peters. After dinner we all went back to Jodie's; we had a few drinks, we laughed, we joked and we shared old times. But, you know, Ryan,' she said, pausing as if the truth were only now dawning on her, 'you're absolutely right—it was a *really* traumatic experience. Yep, no doubt about it; I may never recover.'

He watched her, trying to decide if despite her facetious tone she was giving him the whole story. It was hard to credit that K.C.'s renowned fearlessness could be broken down so easily.

'That's *it*, Ryan,' she stressed. 'I know how your over-protective mind works, but the only unsolicited manhandling I fell victim to last night was yours.'

Blue eyes first flashed at her with anger, then, surprisingly, dulled with hurt. 'You know damn well I'd never hurt you, K.C..'

'Oh, I *know* that, but your trouble is you worry too much about me.'

The mirthless laugh he gave was uncharacteristic. 'Tell me something I don't know, K.C.,' he said.

'OK,' she said, choosing to answer his rhetorical comment because it was easier than dwelling on the fact that he was so close that she could practically feel his body heat. 'I'm no longer the naïve sixteen-year-old you dragged out of the back of Rick Nichols' car all those years ago.'

'Glad to hear it. Though, judging from your recent

boyfriends, your taste in men still leaves a lot to be desired.'

'Maybe, but they're *my* desires, not yours! You have to stop regarding me as some kind of brain-dead bimbo who can't look after herself and is going to fall into the arms of the first smooth-talking male who comes on to her.'

'What makes you think that's how I see you?' he asked with ill-concealed amusement.

'Our past history. If you'd controlled my life any more, Ryan, I'd be in a convent this minute.'

He laughed. 'Kiddo, the only habit you'd ever get into would be a bad one! Besides, you're not Catholic.'

'Honestly, Ryan, trying to have an adult conversation with you is impossible! You're determined to treat me like a child, aren't you?'

'I don't treat you like a child, K.C..'

'No?'

'No.'

'Then perhaps you'd like to tell me why you felt it necessary to wait up until I came home, then?'

His face tensed. 'Because, dammit, as I said last night, I was worried about you. It was late and you hadn't left a note.'

'But how did you know I wasn't home? The car was in the garage.'

'When I checked your room you—'

'You checked my *room*?'

'I look in every night to—'

'To what?' she demanded. 'Tuck me in? Check that I've brushed my teeth and said my prayers? Make sure I'm not entertaining men in my room? For God's sake, Ryan, I'm twenty-four years old! Surely I'm entitled to some privacy even if I am living under your roof?'

'Are you quite finished now?'

'Not by a long shot, buster!'

'Well, too bad, because I've got a few things I'd like to say!'

'Nothing I want to hear!'

Pivoting sharply, she started towards the door, but Ryan whipped an arm out to bar her way, at the same time shifting his position, effectively trapping her between him and the cupboards. She told herself that anger was the only reason her blood was shooting around her body at the speed of light and she tried to hang onto that thought as Ryan's firm male fingers lifted her chin to hold her eyes level with his. His face was only centimetres from hers. She could see the pores in his skin, and the temptation to compare the texture of the tanned smoothness of his forehead with the unshaven masculinity of his jaw had her clenching her hands.

'The only reason I stuck my head in your room, as I do every evening, was to say goodnight, nothing more!'

Ryan silently cursed the fact that K.C.'s temper was such a *physical* thing; every time she so much as sighed impatiently the slinky robe she wore slipped to reveal even more of her small, high breasts.

'Rest assured,' he said drily, 'I'm well aware you're old enough to tuck yourself in and decide whether or not you pray. I'm equally certain your pearly whites are pampered beyond even a dentist's highest standards on a daily basis, and nor do I wish to encroach on either your precious privacy or your love life.'

'Can I have that in writing?'

He continued as if she hadn't spoken. 'However, I do have strict house rules about you bringing men home.'

'Oh, goody, *more* rules! And they are?'

Ryan marvelled that his hands only found their way to her shoulders, despite his inclination to wrap them around her slender, elegant neck. Discussions about sex were the last thing he wanted to get into with K.C., especially when she was clothed only by virtue of a robe and a self-discipline he hadn't known he possessed.

'You *don't* bring them into *my* home. You get it?'

'Not, apparently, while I'm living here,' she retorted. 'Unless you have some in-house deal I haven't heard about.'

'What the hell kind of crack was that?' His eyes scorched her.

'Ryan, I was kidding. I—'

'*Kidding*, K.C.?' He was furious that she could be so naïve. So blasé! Did she think he was made of stone? Hell! His heart was going like a jackhammer and all efforts to shut down the images her remark evoked were being sabotaged by the fact that he was close enough to feel every curve she possessed! He wanted to shake her! Worse, he wanted to step closer, to slide his hand behind her head and guide her delectable little smart-alec mouth of hers under his!

Do it! Do it! his libido urged. Just once. Just taste her once.

'Kidding, K.C.!' he repeated, in the hope of keeping his mouth functioning in safer directions until his common sense checked in again. 'You think it's funny to casually offer your body around, do you? How funny do you think it would be if some guy took you up on the offer? I ought to belt the backside off you!'

'Pass,' she said, starting to turn away. 'That way's too kinky even for me.'

That did it! Telling himself he'd teach her a lesson she'd never forget, Ryan brought his mouth down onto hers. Unfortunately for him, he discovered that K.C. was every teacher's ideal pupil—co-operative, a quick learner and *very* responsive...

CHAPTER FOUR

THERE was only a split second between Kirrily thinking, Oh, God, he's going to kiss me! and the reality of Ryan's lips against hers. In that minuscule time-lapse she assumed that the action would be flavoured with the taste of his anger; she was wrong.

Though surprise had parted her mouth slightly, unlike most men of Kirrily's experience, Ryan was in no hurry to plunge into its depths. Instead his lips moved over hers with soft, individual kisses that were so gentle and tentative that she was expecting every one to be the last and him to step away.

The notion hit her like a sledgehammer and instinctively she rose onto her toes, lifting her arms to his neck to stave off his anticipated retreat. She had no intention of having a kiss she'd imagined for eight long years end after only eight seconds! Spurred on by the electric excitement coiling in her stomach, and the knowledge that with Ryan she always got as good as she gave, Kirrily put everything into her response.

Ryan felt the remnants of his good intentions burn to a crisp as K.C.'s body pressed into his and her teeth nipped at his bottom lip. In weaker moments he'd fantasised about what it would feel like to have K.C.'s active little tongue tracing his mouth, but he'd never expected it to feel as if he was being scorched by a lightning bolt, to feel as if his nervous system had been numb for the past thirty-six years of his life. It was as if she'd found a switch to his emotions, had flicked it from 'off' to 'overdrive' and he was hurtling out of control. The moment of impact came when his tongue touched K.C.'s...

Her legs were going to buckle! Kirrily knew it as surely as she knew that Ryan Talbot was systematically shutting down every one of her vital organs. And, dear God, he was only *kissing* her! She'd been kissed hundreds of times, both personally and professionally, yet nothing had prepared her for the full-scale chaos that her senses were experiencing at Ryan's hands; except he wasn't even using his hands! He was driving her crazy with his mouth and tongue, making her want and ache in the most feminine places, and his hands hadn't yet left her shoulders. It was like being tortured in heaven, simultaneously feeling bliss beyond her dreams and unbearable pain.

She wanted him to touch her—touch her skin, her breasts, her nipples, which felt as if they were going to burst. Her scrambled brain imagined his fingers in a dozen different places all at once and finally, through some miracle of telepathy, they lifted from her shoulders. Desire blazed through her as she anticipated where they would next settle.

When he abandoned her mouth, she moaned in protest, instinctively tightening her arms, confusion and residual sensations of pleasure making her slow to register that no longer was she being embraced but pushed away. But when she opened her eyes the words of puzzlement she'd formed in her mind died a shameful death before they ever left her lips.

'Let go, K.C..'

It wasn't the tone of the command that secured Kirrily's immediate obedience but the look of consummate disgust on Ryan's face; it chilled her as effectively as an Antarctic wind.

'You might think practice makes perfect, K.C., but

I'm not into training apprentices. I like my women old enough to know where they were when Elvis died.'

A thousand witty comebacks surfaced in her brain, but Kirrily couldn't voice one of them. All she could do was stare at the man whose breathing was as ragged as her own but whose eyes looked as if they were made from ice. She wanted to fly at him and punch him until her hands bled. She wanted to rage at him with the force of a hundred cyclones and *still*, more than anything else, she wanted to know what it would be like to have him make love to her, to have him so deep inside her that all she felt was him.

Given what he'd just said, the realisation of how she felt should have sickened her, but instead it lifted her body temperature to a level that on the plus side at least gave her the motivation to salvage her pride.

'*You* started that, Ryan, so don't blame me! And, furthermore, maybe it's about time you did start an apprenticeship scheme,' she said, pleased to see that the suggestion startled him. 'After all, given your *supposed* lay average of six point two five per week, you must've just about *exhausted* the supply of women old enough to remember what they were doing on August the sixteenth, 1977!'

'I was joking about the condoms and you know it!' he snapped.

'Ah, so it's OK for you to joke about sex, but not me, huh? Well, you can take your double standards, Ryan Talbot, and shove them!'

The familiar sound of Jayne's car coming into the drive told Ryan that K.C. was home—an hour later than she should have been.

Cursing, he bench-pressed the weight above his head for the twelfth time, held it longer than he should have, then, gritting his teeth against the ache in his arms, settled it back on the rack above him. He'd acted like an

A-grade jerk, not just in kissing her but in the pathetic way he'd carried on afterwards. But what made him feel even worse was that it was only his 'post kiss' behaviour he felt any genuine regret for, *not* the kiss itself! All day he'd caught himself replaying the scene in his mind and speculating on the possibilities of what would have happened had he not ended it.

'Nice job, Talbot!' he muttered, once again hoisting the weight. 'Don't learn from your…mistakes… embellish the-em with worse…ones!'

Clang!

As the weight dropped into its rack Ryan let his arms flop over the sides of the bench he was lying on. He was exhausted, physically wrung out beyond anything he'd ever felt before, and still he didn't trust himself to walk into the same room as K.C. and not pull her into his arms with the sole purpose of ravishing her. So much for the theory of out of sight, out of mind!

When he'd realised that K.C. was determined to go to the office, he'd decided to work at home so that he could concentrate on the job he was costing and have a final figure to give to the builder. It had been a good plan, except the only figure his brain had been capable of arriving at had been K.C.'s! After two hours of fruitlessly berating his calculator, he'd gone out with the intention of taking a short run to clear his head of her image and his conscience of guilt. Except the jog had ended up as a marathon before he'd admitted the futility of it and resorted to weights. Not that the last four hours in his room working out with those had been much help either. At this rate, if he didn't get his feelings for K.C. under some kind of control it'd be a three-way tie as to what claimed his life first: libido overload, guilt, or heart failure due to extreme physical penance.

He sighed. He owed her an apology. Hell, he owed her his head on a platter with his heart on a stake as an entrée!

'C'mon, Talbot,' he grumbled, getting to his feet. 'It's time to bite the bullet and face the lady.'

Ah! Now there was something he hadn't considered...K.C. might be *armed*, which would present a fourth possible cause of his demise—justifiable homicide!

Kirrily let herself into the house and headed directly for the kitchen. Having slept through breakfast, worked through lunch and kept her focus firmly on invoices all afternoon, she was in immediate, desperate need of both food and caffeine.

Sleep was another commodity she'd have welcomed with open arms, along with an assurance that she'd not have to set eyes on Ryan Talbot until the next life or beyond. Regrettably she was staying in the same house as he was, which was why she'd be going out tonight rather than immediately crawling into her bed. There was no way she was going to spend any more time in his presence than was absolutely unavoidable. In theory that was a sound plan; in reality it stank: he was in the kitchen!

The criminal returns to the scene of the crime, was her first thought. The second was that he'd obviously been working out and that the sheen of perspiration coating his muscles and making his singlet cling to him made him look as sexy as all get out. Remembering her decision to limit herself to one humiliating experience per day, she turned to leave.

'K.C....wait.'

'I don't have time. I—'

'Make time. *Please*... This won't take long.'

She knew that if she kept walking he'd interpret it as running away. Which would be right. One thing she couldn't stand was proving Ryan Talbot right! Fixing a bored expression on her face, she slowly turned, determined to brazen out whatever he had planned.

'K.C., I'm sorry about what happened this morning. I acted like a complete ass. I was way out of line kissing you and…let's be frank, a total bastard for saying what I did afterwards.'

'Look, Ryan, there's no need to beat yourself up over it. It just happened; let's leave it at that.'

'Yeah, but the trouble is, it *shouldn't* have happened. Not like that—*not at all*!' he amended hastily when K.C.'s head jerked up.

'Ryan,' she said, 'I *have* been kissed before.'

'I know that,' he said curtly. 'As you pointed out last night, it was *me* who saved you from Mr Nichols' amorous advances.'

'If you expect my belated thanks, forget it! That was probably the *most* embarrassing moment of my life.' Her eyes narrowed. 'Not only did you split Rick's lip open and scar him for life but for two years no guy was game enough to speak to me, much less make a pass!'

Ryan struggled with a grin. 'Yeah? Well, be grateful it was me and not your father chaperoning that party or they'd still be scraping Nichols' oversexed hide off the road!' The look K.C. gave him was filled with anything but gratitude. Damn! The last thing he wanted was to get into another fight with her. 'Look,' he said, determined to change the subject, 'how about I order some Chinese for dinner and—?'

'Thanks anyway, but I'm going out for dinner.'

'*Again?* With whom?' Ryan wished the words hadn't come out with quite so much irritation. 'I mean, I thought you'd be looking forward to getting an early night.'

'What I'm looking forward to is the fabulous French meal Trevor promised me.'

'You're going out with *Trevor Nichols*? Are you crazy?'

She stiffened at his tone. 'Yes, I'm going out with him and no, I'm not crazy. *I* happen to think he's a nice guy.'

'Did Mr Nice Guy mention he was *married* with *four kids*?'

'Divorced. With three.'

'He's as old as I am!'

'Actually he's older: forty next month.'

'K.C., the guy's way too old for you!'

'For heaven's sake,' Kirrily said, determined to keep her rapidly deteriorating temper in check, 'I'm having dinner with him, not marrying him. It's no big deal.'

'And what about *after* dinner?'

'I don't know. I guess we'll catch a movie or something.'

'Are you *really* that dense?' he asked, looking at her as if she'd lost her mind. 'Trevor Nichols probably has moves Rick could only dream about!'

'So?'

'So call him and cancel.'

Fury thickened her blood, until she was certain it had stopped flowing all together. If Ryan Talbot wasn't the most arrogant, bossy man God had ever put breath into, it wasn't through lack of trying!

'I'll do no such thing!' she said, once she trusted herself to speak. 'I've no intention of sitting home on a Friday night because *you* tell me to. I am—'

'Look,' he said, 'if it'll make you feel any better *I'll* take you out to dinner.'

He made it sound like the ultimate in noble sacrifices. The rat!

'Thanks, but no thanks. As I've just explained, I'm having dinner with Trev.'

'And *I've* explained that good old *Trev* is *my* age and has the hormones of a lusty eighteen-year-old!' he said, looking at her as if she were a particularly dull child. 'Good God, K.C.! Doesn't that tell you *anything*?'

'Well, of course it does,' she said, and produced her best wide-eyed smile. 'It tells me to stay on my toes if he starts quizzing me on where I was when the king of rock 'n' roll died!'

Ryan's mood for the next hour was such that even Major gave him a wide berth, but, dammit, the idea of Trevor Nichols hitting on K.C. had his gut tied in knots. Yeah, sure, Nichols had only gone into the office to pay off his account. The guy had had an unsealed credit limit for years!

It wasn't that he didn't like Nichols—in most circumstances he was a decent guy—but Ryan had pretty much grown up with the bloke and knew how his mind ticked when it came to beautiful women. The way he figured it, around K.C. Nichols was going to be a veritable time bomb! And the moment the doorbell chimed Ryan was on his feet...

'I'll get it, K.C.!' he yelled.

'G'day, Ryan,' Trevor greeted him, seemingly immune to Ryan's ungracious grunt and scathing look. 'How's business?'

'Terrific, Nichols,' Ryan replied, motioning him inside. 'That account you paid today really turned things around.'

The other man laughed. 'You know me, mate—like to stay on top of things.'

Before he realised that the man's choice of words had been unintentional Ryan's fist clenched and it took enormous restraint on his part to uncurl his fingers and lead him through to the living room.

'Kirri was saying Jayne's gone overseas,' Nichols said conversationally.

Ryan nearly gagged. *Kirri?* Kirri and *Trev*! 'Struth! It was enough to make a weaker man spew! Almost enough reason to close down a construction company's line of credit! Recognising that his thinking was in danger of slipping from that of a part-time idiot to a full-time lunatic, he managed to limit his reaction to an affirmative grunt. Still, he couldn't resist saying, 'Knowing *Kirrily*, she'll be ages yet; can I get you a drink while you're waiting?'

'Wrong, Ryan!'

Both men turned at the sound of K.C.'s voice, watching, mute, as she swanned into the room wearing a full-length black woollen cape.

'Hi, Trev,' she said, giving her escort a dazzling smile. 'As you can see, contrary to the bad press you've been hearing, I'm ready, but feel free to have a drink if you want.'

It was no surprise to Ryan that Nichols declined. He was so blatantly anxious to get K.C. alone that Ryan figured he'd have passed on the drink even if it had included a complimentary million bucks. Not that Ryan could blame him; K.C. was made up like an eastern princess! She'd done her eyes in a way that turned their innocent, doe-like tilt into a sultry, seductive slant and coloured her lips with something that made them look temptingly wet. Her long curtain of hair was held back on one side by a gold and pearl clip, thus displaying a gold earring that glittered and tinkled with the slightest movement of her head. To say that she was beautiful was the understatement of the century.

'Trev,' she said, 'does your car have a heater?'

'Well, er…yeah. Yeah, it does.'

'Great! That means I won't need this cumbersome coat!'

She started shrugging out of the garment as she spoke, the end result of the exercise leaving her standing in the shortest, tightest creation that Ryan had ever seen. It clung to her like a second skin although, unlike skin, it gave him serious doubts as to whether a person could possibly sit down in it! Forget that it was long-sleeved and had a polo-neck; if it didn't fall into the category of indecent then it sure as hell ought to qualify as illegal!

While Ryan stood immobilised, trying to get a grip on emotions too numerable to list, K.C. fired another hundred-megawatt smile in the direction of her date. 'Won't be a sec; I'll just put this away.'

Clearly devoid of the ability to speak, the man merely nodded as K.C.'s long, black-nylon-clad legs carried her out of the room.

Ryan was torn between the desire to follow her and demand she change into something else—preferably sackcloth and ashes—and the need to set the drooling *Trev* straight on a few ground rules. The knowledge he'd be wasting his breath on K.C. made up his mind.

'Listen, Nichols,' he said, moving to stand toe to toe with the other man. 'You so much as *think* about laying one hand on her and I swear to God what I did to your brother will look like a love pat compared to what I'll do to you. You got that? You take her out, you feed her and you bring her home. End of story.'

'Kirri may have other ideas—'

'Then make bloody sure *you* don't!'

The look of appreciation which spread across the man's face as he looked towards the door was all Ryan needed to see to know that K.C. had reappeared. Stepping aside, he forced what he doubted would pass as a smile and muttered an insincere comment about enjoying their meal.

'I'm sure we will,' K.C. answered, slipping her arm through Nichols' and smiling up at him. 'By the way, Ryan,' she said, arching a perfect eyebrow, 'will you by any chance be waiting up for me?'

Gritting his teeth, he looked to the other man. 'No, K.C., I'm certain you won't come to any harm with Trevor.'

'OK. So long as I know what to expect when I walk in tonight.' Ignoring the puzzled looks Nichols was sending both of them, Ryan gave her a saccharine smile.

'I promise that this time the lights will be on and that Major will be your only welcoming committee.'

'So what's causing the trouble between you and Talbot?' Trevor Nichols asked Kirrily as they pulled away from the kerb.

'Only a chronic case of overprotectiveness,' she said, trying to tug her dress down to at least mid-thigh. 'He considers me a child and so constantly treats me like some kind of wayward kid sister.'

'Yeah, right.'

'No, really. He's been like that ever since my brother died; he can't seem to get it through his thick head that I'm a big girl now.'

Trevor sent her a sideways glance. 'You do realise it's because he loves you, don't you?'

'Oh, I know that! But he loves Jayne too and he doesn't try to run her life the way he does mine.'

'What I mean is that he's *in love* with you.'

For the first time since he'd called to collect her Trevor Nichols had Kirrily's full and complete attention. 'You must be crazy if you think that!'

'Maybe,' he said. 'But I'm not stupid, Kirri.' He turned, giving her a wry smile. 'In future when you ask a bloke out with the intention of using him for bait, at least do him the favour of letting him know you're fishing for piranha!'

CHAPTER FIVE

TREVOR NICHOLS might well have been the most charming, entertaining date that Kirrily had ever had, but she'd been so preoccupied with her own thoughts that it was equally possible he had been an obnoxious lout who'd stripped naked and danced on the table between courses.

'What I mean is that he's in love with you...' 'In love with you...' 'In love with you...' 'In love with you...'

As they had done all night, Trevor's words continued to reverberate through Kirrily's mind into the pre-dawn hours, keeping her from sleep—not because she gave them any credence, but because they were forcing her, for the first time, to analyse *her* feelings for Ryan. Only, the more she tried to dissect her emotions, the more confused and...more *worried* she became.

Was it possible she was in love with Ryan?

No! she couldn't be. She didn't *want* to be.

Ryan Talbot was the most patronising, bossy, over-protective man she'd ever known and there was no way she could love such a person. Well, sure... OK, she loved him, but in the same way she loved her folks and Jayne and Bob and Pam Talbot—like family! And while it was true she'd suffered crushes on Ryan over the years so had most of her friends. Heck, he was gorgeous to look at, had a body to die for and a smile that could melt bones at a hundred paces! What normal, red-blooded teenage girl wouldn't have had a crush on him?

Well and good, her brain agreed, but how do you account for the fact that now you are twenty-four he can still get you all hot and bothered just by looking at you? And why was your heart spinning out of control when he kissed you the other day?

Hormones! she rationalised. Pure, unadulterated *lust*. Just because she'd got older it didn't mean she'd become blind to Ryan's sex appeal. And if she was more susceptible to it than she'd been at sixteen it was only because she was at an age where she was more attuned to her own sexuality.

OK, her brain kicked in again, but you're in a business where sexy, good-looking hunks are as common as ice is to the North Pole. How come you don't have the same reaction to them?

Because…well, because I'm already connected to Ryan on an emotional level, she argued with herself. It's like being sad when an acquaintance dies but devastated when a relative dies— The realisation that she might one day lose Ryan jerked her upright in the bed, heart pounding.

She'd been nine the night she'd rushed from her bed in reaction to the banshee wails of her mother, only to learn that her brother, Steven, had been killed. For a long time she'd been haunted by the utter sense of loss, helplessness and confusion she'd felt as everyone around her, especially Jayne, fell victim to the venom of unexpected death. Countless times during her teenage years she'd lain awake and forced herself to imagine losing one or both of her parents in similar circumstances, tearfully resolving that never again would the Grim Reaper catch her off guard.

With the reasoning of youth, she determined that, having experienced her brother's death and by training herself to expect the worst, when she was again confronted with the mortality of those she loved she would, to some degree at least, be insulated from the pain. And so she'd visualised her life without her parents and grandparents, without Jayne, even without Russia, the family dog…

But never, *never* had she tried to visualise her life without Ryan. Until now.

'No. No,' she whispered thickly. 'I can't begin to imagine what it would be like without him.' But the truth was that she *could*; it felt as if someone was piercing her heart with a shard of jagged metal.

The sound of wheels scraping over the ground behind him intruded on the steady rhythm of Ryan's trainers hitting the pathway; instinctively he veered onto the grass, allowing the rollerblader to breeze past him. He wondered if the skater was a genuine fitness fanatic who thought lying in bed on a cold, damp Saturday morning was a crime or if the guy, like himself, was ignoring the chill and threatening rain in the hope that physical fatigue would grant what his conscience hadn't during the night—the respite of sleep.

Even after hearing Kirrily come home at the respectable time of eleven forty-two he hadn't been able to get to sleep and he'd had to admit that it was a lot more than brotherly concern keeping him awake. It was his libido—dammit! Anger at himself spurred his pace and, glancing down at his feet, he wondered how many kilometres they would run before he got himself back on an even keel.

It was his own fault, of course; he should never have kissed her. Yeah, that had to qualify as the biggest mistake in mankind's history, right after the fiasco with the apple in Eden; but hell, he understood how temptation could have overpowered poor old Adam! Even now he only had to run his tongue across his teeth and he could taste her sweetness—

Catching himself enacting the thought, Ryan swore and again increased his pace. Had any other woman ever affected him the way K.C. did? Had he ever wanted one as much? He swore again when the answer on both counts was no. *Never!*

Yet it wasn't merely the strength of the physical attraction that K.C. evoked that bothered him, it was the way she'd unbalanced his emotions, as if every feeling he experienced was somehow linked to her. Sure, he'd always cared for K.C. and shared a special bond with her, but now it seemed that the dimensions of that bond had altered, swung more heavily in her favour. Ryan wished for the power magically to make K.C. fifteen again, just long enough for him to get a fix on exactly how she'd made him feel back then.

'Idiot!' he chided. All the wishful thinking in the world wasn't going to alter the fact that K.C. was now an incredibly beautiful woman and that his emotional disorientation was created by lust. The more he saw of her, the harder it was to remember her as the little kid who'd trailed around after Steve, Jayne and him, chanting, 'Take me or I'll tell Mum and Dad!'

'Take me'! Geez, could his warped mind give those words a whole different slant! And again he picked up the pace of his stride.

Despite the onset of a persistent drizzle, Ryan continued his physical punishment for another ninety minutes, urged on by frustration and the cowardly hope that by the time he finally went home K.C. might have gone out. At some stage during his solo marathon, he came to the conclusion that his only chance of avoiding further potentially embarrassing scenes with K.C. lay in steering clear of situations where they would be alone together. Finally, drenched by both sweat and rain, he turned into his street, grateful that there was only tomorrow and then Monday and the start of five days where, surrounded by work colleagues, he could distract his hormones without having to pump iron or risk running himself to death.

As for the evenings, well, he'd spent three nights last week deliberately losing at poker with the two geriatric cleaners who came in after hours and if necessary he'd do the same again this week. While the old guys were

bound to tell all and sundry how they'd fleeced him for
a hefty amount of cash, Ryan would rather be regarded
as a pathetically bad gambler than be the cause of any
more stress for K.C..

The sight of the police car parked about a hundred
metres up ahead drew a groan from him. Obviously the
Dunford kid was in strife, *again*. It had been a month
since Ryan's elderly neighbour had asked him to have a
word with her fourteen-year-old grandson, in the hope
that the kid might heed a man when he wouldn't listen
to her. After four trouble-free weeks, Ryan had started
thinking that young Sean had meant what he'd said
about channelling his artistic ability into something more
productive than painting murals on the walls of the local
council chambers.

Cursing the stupidity of youth, he jogged down his
neighbour's flower-edged drive and around to the back
door, where he knocked loudly.

'Mrs Dunford! It's me, Ryan.'

Almost immediately, a well-dressed, grey-haired
woman opened the door. Wiping water from his face
with an equally wet hand, Ryan gave her a rueful smile.
'What's he done this time?'

The look on the old lady's face indicated that the entire incident was beyond her comprehension. Ryan
wanted to rip the kid's ears off for causing the woman
so much grief. 'Would it help, Mrs Dunford, if I came
in and talked to the police?'

Her wrinkled brow squashed up even more. 'Ryan,
the police aren't *here*,' she said. 'They went into *your*
place.'

'*My* place?'

'Yes. They—'

Without waiting to hear more Ryan dashed across the
soggy yard and, using Mrs Dunford's barbecue as a
springboard, vaulted the eight-foot fence dividing their

properties. He only just managed to keep his footing as he landed, but with scant regard for the slick pavement surrounding the pool he sprinted to the back patio and wrenched open the kitchen door.

'K.C.!' he bellowed, not caring that Major scooted out as he entered. 'K.C., where are you?'

Kirrily didn't even have time to answer before Ryan's wet, dripping bulk was filling the entrance of the sun room. He became statue-still as his eyes locked on the two grim-faced police officers present, and she knew exactly what he was thinking and feeling; she'd felt the same way when she'd opened the door and seen the uniforms.

'They're OK, Ryan,' she said quickly, almost able to taste his dread. 'Nothing's happened to them.'

It seemed to take a second for her words to register with him, then the extent of his relief was evident in the way he slumped against the doorframe. 'Thank God,' he muttered.

His words, too, were identical to hers when she had learned that her worst fears—that something had happened to her family—were unfounded. But the relief of knowing that her parents were safe, which had initially insulated her from the shock of learning the real reason for the police visit, now seemed to be wearing off. Though she read the request for an explanation in Ryan's eyes she was devoid of the ability to know where to begin. It didn't make sense! It was crazy!

Although Ryan's pulse-rate had slowed somewhat, K.C.'s pale, shell-shocked expression and the presence of two cops in his house was enough to keep it above its regular tempo.

'OK,' he said, moving further into the room. 'Someone want to tell me what's going on?'

'Sir, I'm Sergeant Stuart.' The smaller of the two men spoke. 'And this is Constable Ellard.'

'Ryan Talbot. What's the problem, Sergeant?'

'The Victoria police requested we contact Ms Cosgrove on their behalf.'

Ryan tensed. 'Why?'

'Sir, the—'

'There's been a fire,' K.C. cut in. Eyes wide with disbelief, she hugged herself tightly. 'My house h...has been burned.'

Ryan swore. Though he'd never seen the house, he knew how damn much it meant to her, how proud she was of it.

'Ah, hell, honey, I'm sorry.' Grimacing at the inadequacy of the words, he took a step towards her with the intention of pulling her into his arms, but she eluded him.

'How could someone set fire to my house?' she asked, looking lost as she wandered in a small, tight circle by the window. 'How could a person do that? Why *me*? What have I done to deserve this...this *hate*?'

The fear and terror he saw in her face made his heart ache, and this time he gave her no chance to evade him. One stride brought him close enough to still her agitated body and, ignoring the fact he was drenched, he wrapped an arm around her, drawing her to him.

'Honey,' he said, tilting her chin until her too shiny eyes met his and gently slipping a strand of hair behind her left ear, 'listen to me. A fire isn't personal; it didn't start because of anything you have or haven't done. These things happen. It might have been an electrical fault or something, but it...' He paused, catching sight of the sergeant's slowly shaking head. A chill snaked down his spine at the copper's expression; instinctively he tightened his hold of K.C..

'It wasn't an electrical fault, Mr. Talbot.' Ryan read the cop's pause as a silent warning of what was to come.

'As I've told Ms Cosgrove, according to the fire inspector, the blaze was deliberately lit.'

'Delib— Who the hell by?' Ryan demanded.

'Presumably by the stalker who's been harassing Ms Cosgrove the last few months.'

'*What?*'

CHAPTER SIX

ONCE K.C. began recounting the events of her last few months in Melbourne, Ryan's anger swelled with such intensity that he thought it would choke him. Hell, it was only the presence of the police which kept him from leaping from his seat and *choking* K.C.!

She'd been the victim of hate mail, death threats and a car bombing and had kept it to herself! Cripes, she hadn't even had the common sense to get the hell out of Melbourne! Now her house had been fire-bombed, and had it not been for her loyalty to Jayne she'd probably be dead. How could she have treated these events in such a blasé manner? What had she been thinking? Nothing, obviously! If stupidity were rewarded in the afterlife, Ryan figured that God was already preparing quite a reception for Kirrily Cosgrove!

Even now, an hour later, fury was still searing through Ryan's body, and in the absence of the police it was taking every bit of self-control he possessed to keep it checked. The urge to wrench her from her seat at the table and shake her until she admitted to her idiocy was overwhelming. Damn, she'd been in serious danger and not done a bloody thing about it, not even *told* him about it!

Yet the recriminations which rose to his tongue remained there unspoken. Letting fly with a tirade of abuse might make *him* feel better, but it was clearly the last thing K.C. needed. Her wan expression and detached, overly composed behaviour warned him to tread warily.

Since the police had left she'd retreated further behind a façade of calm normality more suited to a robot than a flesh-and-blood person, and completely alien to the vivaciousness which personified Kirrily Cosgrove.

Ryan had never seen her look so emotionally fragile and for that reason he was determined to bite his tongue rather than be the trigger which sent her over the edge. But then again…perhaps it might be better to prod her temper, to get her stirred up enough so she released the feelings she was so obviously trying to hold in. Yeah, he thought. Maybe that was the way to deal with this.

Aw, damn it, Talbot! he chided himself silently. Admit you don't have a bloody clue about how to handle things, that the only other time you felt so freaking useless was when you watched her brother die!

His insides iced at the reminder of how easily K.C. could have been killed in the fire. Looking across at her slumped shoulders and bent head, he clenched his fists, wanting nothing more than five minutes alone with the bastard who was doing this to her, to make the creep pray for the luxury of a slow and painful death.

'I'll have to get the first available flight to Melbourne.'

K.C.'s statement jerked him from his bloodthirsty thoughts, disbelief propelling him from the sink to the kitchen table.

'*What?*' he demanded, but she gave no indication that she was even aware of his presence, much less his angry incredulousness. He moved until he was standing directly in front of her, but her gaze remained focused on the cup of coffee she'd nursed for nearly forty minutes without once lifting it to her mouth.

Reminding himself to stay calm, he dragged back a chair, turning it so that he could straddle it. 'K.C., look at me,' he urged gently, then gritted his teeth when she still refused to acknowledge him. 'Honey, you've had a shock and you're not thinking clearly. There's no reason for you to go to Melbourne—'

'There is.' Her head lifted and she stared at him with vague green eyes. 'I've a million things to take care of down there. I think I should deal with the insurance angle first, though...'

Her soft voice, so devoid of emotion, scared the hell out of him. The K.C. he knew should have been screaming her desire for revenge on top note, not accepting events with limp docility.

'Yes, I'll do that first,' she continued calmly, once again addressing the cup, 'call the insurance comp— No. I can't; it's Saturday. I'll...I'll do it...not tomorrow...the next day. I guess I could call Carole... I haven't talked to her for a week. She might have some work for me. A script to look at or—'

She stopped when he prised the cup from her hands. The coldness of her fingers made him trap them in his in the hope of warming them.

'Listen,' he said. 'Why don't you go lie down for a while? Get some rest and—'

'I don't have time to just lie around, Ryan!' Wrenching herself free of his grasp as if scalded, she glared at him. 'In case you don't get the picture here, some lunatic has destroyed my home and I've got to go back to Melbourne!'

'Why?' he asked, with a patience he was far from feeling.

'Because I...' She faltered as if she wasn't sure herself, before hurriedly shoving her chair from the table and standing. 'Because I need to see the extent of the damage, talk to the police, see if Cathy and Paul are OK—'

'K.C.!'

Realising he'd raised his voice, he stopped and drew a long, steadying breath. 'The police already told you— the house has been totalled. Cathy and Paul were both away and are perfectly safe. Look,' he said, 'you can talk to the cops, the fire department and any other devil you want by *phone* but you can't go—'

'I can and *will* do anything I like, Ryan! Nobody controls me! Not you, not anyone! So quit playing big brother and bossing me around like you've got a right to!'

'I'm not *playing* at anything, K.C.! I'm trying to *protect* you.'

'Well, don't!' she screamed at him. 'I don't want your bloody protection! I—'

The sight of her battling tears made Ryan's chest cramp. 'Ah, sheesh, honey! C'mere…'

'Leave me alone!' She backed to the door, an arm outstretched to ward him off. 'I mean it, Ryan. Ju-just let me be.'

'K.C., please… I only want to help y—'

'Fine. Then call the airport and get me on…a f-f-flight. I'm going to pack!'

She pivoted round and raced into the hallway, and within seconds her bedroom door slammed.

Standing in the damp chill of Melbourne's dwindling winter twilight, Kirrily felt as if she was existing in some sort of warped dream or playing a role in a far-fetched television drama. Grasping the cool wrought-iron of her front gate, she stared at what remained of her recently painted weatherboard home, trying to accept what its charred remains represented, trying to comprehend that another human being wanted to kill her.

Her stomach rolled and lurched and there was nothing she could do to stop its contents from emptying at the base of the nearby rose bush. Spots danced before her eyes as she recalled how she'd started tending the bush, eagerly awaiting the spring to discover what colour its flowers would be, imagining how their scent would drift up to her veranda on the gentle evening breeze and how pleasant it would be to sit there studying her lines—

The futility of such thoughts now brought on another wave of nausea. Though the plant was untouched by the devastation which had taken place twenty metres away, there was no longer a veranda for her to sit on. The bull-nosed iron awning lay with ugly deformity across the pathway leading from the front gate—a pathway which now led to nothing more than the charred skeleton of her house and her dream. Come spring, the rose bush would bloom on a vacant block of land. She retched again, but her stomach had nothing left to surrender.

'C'mon, honey, let's go—'

She jerked away from the hand which gently touched her shoulder; gentleness didn't belong in this scene. Pulling a handful of tissues from her coat pocket, she blotted her mouth then straightened, gulping in air still carrying the stench of smoke.

Why was it that her life always seemed more screwed up than anyone else's? Why was it that one complication cropped up after another? Ryan always claimed that as a teenager she'd gone out of her way to look for trouble; perhaps she had, but ironically it seemed that trouble now followed her around.

She found herself fighting to hold back laughter at the accuracy of that thought—these days Ryan Talbot had become trouble personified and he'd damn well insisted on shadowing her all the way from Sydney! Yet she had only to look at the destruction in front of her to realise that the physical and emotional threat Ryan Talbot presented to her was aeons away from the danger represented by the nameless, faceless person who'd done this.

Again irony slapped her in the face as she studied the two remaining exterior walls of what had been her home; some bizarre twist of fate was giving her almost the exact opposite of what she craved. She was obsessed with Ryan, a builder and architect, yet she had become the obsession of some maniac who'd ultimately destroyed her house.

Oh, Kirrily, she thought, feeling a sick desire to laugh, if your life gets weirder they'll commission Dean Koontz to write your life story!

She pushed at the gate and it swung silently open, testament to the copious amounts of oil she'd fed it to stop it squealing like a stuck pig. But her memories of the smiling real-estate agent quickly dismissing the noise as 'easily curable' and steering her along the path that day she'd first inspected the house were banished by the discouraging hand clamping down on her shoulder.

'No, K.C.! It's not safe. The whole place could come down in a second.'

Heedless of both the words and the fire department signs endorsing them, Kirrily shrugged free. No one would tell her what to do in her own home. *No one!* She was an adult. An intelligent, hard-working, independent adult who'd proved that she could stand on her own two feet, even living hundreds of miles from her family and everything she'd grown up with, and *survive*. On her *own* and in *her own* home.

'Honey, stop. You can't go any further.'

This time the tone and grip accompanying the command were stronger, prompting her to lash out verbally and physically.

'I *can*!' she screamed. 'I can do anything I damn well please, Ryan Talbot! Damn it—let go of me!'

Ryan was quick enough to pull his head out of the way of her left hook so that it did little more than graze his ear, but its sting was enough to tell him that she hadn't pulled her punch. That K.C. never did sent relief washing through him even as her booted foot connected with his shin; thank God she was starting to react normally! Despite his relief, though, Ryan's instincts for self-preservation kicked in and his superior height enabled him to wrap a leg around K.C.'s in time to inhibit a second direct hit.

'Settle down, hon; it's OK. Everything's going to be OK.'

She told him what she thought of that with one succinct word. 'Nothing's *ever* OK!' she raged. 'Life is a bitch! A rotten, stinking screwed up—'

'Yeah, honey, I know. I know—'

'You think you know everything, Ryan Talbot!' she screeched, squirming to get free. 'Well, you don't!'

Ryan could not only feel her anger but he could see it, banking higher and higher in her bright green eyes, and he refused to release her. He prayed her fury would quickly give way to the tears she'd been fighting all day; she needed the emotional release of a good cry.

'Let it go, K.C.,' he urged gently. 'You need to get it ou—'

'Damn it, don't tell me wha—' Her words choked off as her face contorted and she fought to swallow the sob Ryan heard in her voice. He made no attempt to stop the short, sharp punches she rained on his chest.

'Hey, mate! You want I should keep hangin' round here? The meter's still tickin'.'

Ryan glanced across at the cab they'd taken direct from the airport. He was reluctant to drag K.C. kicking and screaming through a hotel lobby, thus making her the next cover story for every celebrity tabloid in the country; on the other hand it was now dark, and getting colder by the second.

'A few minutes, mate!' he told the driver, readjusting his hold on K.C. who, although still fighting *him*, was at least focusing her verbal abuse on whoever had set fire to her home.

'Kill the bastard! How dare he do this…to my house? It's not fair… It's not one stinking bit fair!' she sobbed, pounding her fist into his shoulder. 'I *loved* that house! It was my independence.' She flayed at his body. 'I bought that house…all by myself, without consulting

Dad or Mum or…or without one bit of your…your precious advice or *protection*…or…or *anything*.'

She punched him again and again, but the intensity of the blows lessened in direct ratio to the increased strength of her crying. 'I…I…loved that house, Ryan. I d-did; I really, really did…'

'Shh, sweetheart, I know,' he crooned. 'I know.'

Finally even her voice was drowned in her tears. Strangely, though, while her physical assault on him had been heartfelt on her part, for Ryan it had carried no real sting; yet as his body absorbed the distressed shudders of her tiny, fragile frame it felt as if his heart and guts were being ripped out piece by tiny piece.

The intensity of what he was feeling stunned him, for it went beyond any physical pain he'd ever experienced, ever imagined. He understood that sympathy for another could run deep, but this was different. More different than he could comprehend.

It was as if he was hurting *with* K.C. not *for* her, as if her personal pain belonged equally to him. And it burned more cruelly than any he'd ever known, even more than what he'd felt when his best friend had died in his arms.

CHAPTER SEVEN

KIRRILY took one glimpse at herself in the bathroom mirror and turned away, groaning; she looked like hell on a bad day and felt worse.

Opening the one, hastily packed piece of luggage she'd brought, she pulled out an old, faded green sweatsuit. The outfit had never flattered her, but Kirrily figured that there wasn't a designer alive who could minimise the effects of what she'd gone through today. Stepping into the sweatpants, she directed mumbled obscenities at the mongrel who'd burned her home, but it wasn't until she was pulling the sweatshirt over her head that the enormity of what she'd lost hit her full force. She froze, reality not just biting but ravishing her right through to her bones.

The house and its contents were insured and could be replaced, with new, probably nicer versions, but what of her truly personal possessions: her school records, her grandmother's jewellery, the photographs of her and her brother—the items that had radiated love and cherished memories? Those things were gone for ever, as irreplaceable as Steven himself. Too numb even to cry, she stood motionless, trying to make sense of everything.

In in the last few weeks her marginally less than mundane life had begun resembling the lead role in a full-length Hollywood horror flick. And yet even now, despite all evidence to the contrary, she couldn't entirely accept that someone was trying to kill her.

It didn't make sense.

'No!' There *had* to be another explanation. 'Someone might want to *scare* me, make my life a misery or just plain tick me off, but no one—*no one*—could have a valid reason for wanting to kill me!'

She was unaware she'd shouted the denial until Ryan burst into her bedroom.

'What is it, what's wrong?' he demanded, rushing across the room to grasp her arms.

'N-n-nothing. I was just thinking aloud. I'm OK.'

The fear tensing the muscles in his gut eased immediately, but those in his chest tightened at the confusion and fatigue etched in her face. Though she'd slept for the better part of five hours her eyes remained slightly puffy and red from crying. Gently he lifted the long strand of wet hair clinging to her cheek and hooked it behind her ear. 'You don't look it. Feeling a bit better?'

For a moment she stared at him as if she couldn't recognise him, then swallowed and nodded uncertainly. To Ryan the fact that she hadn't been baited by his unintentional insult or grasped the opportunity to point out that under the circumstances his question was a dumb one only highlighted exactly how strung out she was. Sighing at his inability to do anything to catch the animal who was doing this to her, he released her and stepped back.

When he let go of her, Kirrily found it required a concentrated effort on her part simply to remain standing. In the insanity of the fire and the knee-jerk trip from Sydney, she'd forgotten all about Ryan. Well, not about *him* per se—only that last night she'd realised she was in love with him—but when he'd burst through the door, clad only in jeans and looking every bit the concerned, rescuing hero, her heart had gone into melt-down. *Her heart and every other organ in her body.*

She couldn't exactly recall when she'd last seen him without a shirt, but she sure as hell knew that whenever it had been he hadn't looked like *this*. An encounter with

anything *this* spectacular was something a woman would
remember like her own birthday! Hastily she averted her
eyes from the muscled bareness of his chest. Oh, God,
her life was getting more like a bad movie by the minute! Not only was someone threatening her, but as a sub-
plot she was in love with a guy who wasn't the least bit
interested. She could even visualise the press release:
Kirrily— The tale of a woman pursuing a hopeless love
and pursued by a faceless terror!

'What's so funny?' Ryan asked, first startled then
worried by the sudden mirthless laugh she gave.

'My life,' she quipped, dropping artlessly onto the
bed. 'Or at least my existence in this parallel universe.'

A considering expression crossed her face. 'You think
that's what could've happened, Ryan? That I've somehow crossed over into a parallel universe? I mean, it
makes as much sense as everything else that's happened.'

'Nothing about this makes sense to me, K.C., least of
all why you kept this business to yourself.'

His determined expression left her no hope of side-
stepping an explanation. She sighed.

'Apart from the fact it was my business, I didn't tell
Mum and Dad because I knew they'd either camp on
my doorstep or try and haul me back to Sydney.' Or
send you to do it, she added silently.

'You shouldn't have needed *hauling back*; you
should've had the brains to leave the minute this all
started,' he argued. 'Staying down here alone was the
most *stupid, idiotic* thing you've ever done.'

'Well, thank you so much for pointing out that I've
scored a personal best. But, if you recall, I've been in
Sydney over a week! We flew back today. Remember?'

'We flew back because a nut case, *who has been harassing you for months*, set fire to your house! He also
blew up your car! Anyone with *half* a brain would have
headed for Sydney *then*. Anyone with a *functioning*

brain would have got out after the first couple of hate
letters turned up in their mailbox!'

'Well, then, the entire cast of *Hot Heaven* must be
brainless because *everyone* got hate letters,' she informed him. 'Even the scriptwriters and producers, and
none of them left town! Are you going to personally
abuse every one of them too?'

'I don't care about them!' He swore violently. 'Damn
it, K.C., they aren't in danger—*you are.*'

'Well, yes, even someone as stupid as I apparently am
can recognise that *now*. But until today not even the
police thought the threats were directed to me personally.'

He sent her a look of utter disbelief. 'Get real, K.C.;
your car was blown *sky-high*!'

Did he really think she was such an imbecile that
she'd have stuck around if she'd been convinced that the
attack had been deliberately aimed at her? Judging by
the way he was glaring at her, he did. Yep, no doubt
about it, Ryan Talbot had her at the top of his list entitled
'People Who Need Lobotomies'! Then again, considering the way she felt about him, *knowing* of his low opinion of her, who was she to argue?

She dismissed the idea of wasting her breath on refusing to discuss the matter and ordering him from the
room. He wouldn't go and, in all honesty, she needed to
talk, preferably to someone who'd listen rather than lecture, but Ryan was all she had.

'The car was a loaner,' she started. 'An advertising
promotion by *Hot Heaven*'s main sponsor. Six of us on
the show drove the exact same make, model and colour.
It could have belonged to any one of us.' After muttering
something under his breath, Ryan sat down only inches
from her bare feet.

'Start at the beginning,' he said.

Drawing her knees to her chest and hugging them as
a defence against the insane urge to touch his beautifully

muscled arm, she expelled a resigned sigh. 'Over the years *Hot Heaven* has periodically been targeted by extreme moralists plus the usual assorted nuts,' she said. 'Hate mail and threatening calls to the network weren't exactly new and no big deal. It got worse when my previously lily-white character, Skye, began an affair with her best friend's blind father, the general trend of complaints being that the show was a corrupting influence and getting really tacky.'

'*Getting* tacky?' Ryan raised a questioning eyebrow. 'You mean there was a time when it *wasn't*?'

'Listen, Ryan,' she said heatedly, bouncing onto her knees, 'no one claimed it was award-winning drama, but it was steady, well-paid work! I liked it and, judging by the ratings, so did the audiences.'

'Not everyone, apparently.'

'But that's what I don't get!' She eased back onto her heels. 'Why would a person keep watching a programme they dislike? I mean, no one's forcing them to do it. No one compels them to tune in twice a week. There are plenty of other channels they could watch.'

'Yes,' he said. 'I guess there are.'

The searching look he gave her made Kirrily feel as if her blood had caught fire, as if a current of electricity was arcing from his blue eyes and immobilising her.

'Then again,' he said, still holding her gaze, 'there are reasons other than first-class dialogue and plot that attract and hook viewers.'

'Such…as?' she managed to ask, pulse hammering.

'Such as the need to look for something to complain about.'

'Oh…I thought you meant—' She stopped dead, knowing she'd come close to making herself look an even bigger idiot. Yeah, right, like he's going to say you!

'Thought I meant what?' he pushed, an irritated edge to his tone.

'Nothing,' she said, pulling a lint ball from the knee

of her sweatpants. 'It's not hard to work out *you* considered the programme beneath *your* intellect.'

'I'd have assumed it was below that of any thinking person.' He practically grunted with distaste. 'In my opinion it's little more than gratuitous sex and sleaze.'

'Aha! You *do* watch it!'

The muscles in his jaw tensed. 'My opinion's based on the promotions the channel does and what I've heard from Jayne. *She* watches it. Presumably out of some inane sense of loyalty to you.'

'My mistake,' she said. 'Obviously, as your views of the show are based on such *extensive* long-term study of it, then they must be right. *As usual!*'

'Listen,' he said wearily, 'let's not get into an argument about the supposed merits of a show even you didn't think enough of to re-sign for. I—'

'The only reason I didn't re-sign was because I wasn't offered a contract!' On seeing his genuine surprise, Kirrily wished she'd kept her mouth shut.

'You mean they sacked you?'

'I wasn't *sacked*.' The way she shifted her eyes before adding feebly, 'They just didn't want to renegotiate my contract,' told Ryan that there was more to it.

'Why?' he asked, repeating the question when she remained silent and her attention stayed on the worn knees of her pants. '*Why*, K.C.?'

'I don't know.' She shrugged, head bent. 'They probably just wanted—'

He lifted her chin, returning her steely glare with one of his own and refusing to speculate on why her stubbornness left him feeling challenged rather than irritated. 'Why, K.C.?'

She jerked her head free, the mattress bouncing as she jumped off the bed. 'You always have to know *everything*, don't you?' It was a complaint, not a question. 'All right, then!' she continued. 'It was because certain people at the network said I was difficult to work with and temperamental. Which is a load of—'

'Sounds credible to me,' he muttered.

'Listen, Ryan,' she fumed, her temper restoring much needed colour to her cheeks, 'compared to some cast members, Mother Theresa's got nothing on me.'

'Not that your role ever called for you to have much on.'

'Oh, shut up!'

She snatched up a hairbrush and began dragging it through her damp hair in a way that made him wince. After several strokes the anger went out of her and her hands fell dejectedly to her sides. He waited out the ensuing minutes of strained silence by watching her reflection in the mirror and trying to interpret the dozens of emotions that flickered in her face. Eventually, she became aware of his interest. The visual connection caused a hot flaring deep inside him.

'The real reason I was canned was because I made a bad career decision.' The mirror reflected her rueful face. 'I refused to move in with the network manager's son.'

Kirrily could have predicted Ryan's raised eyebrow reaction, but the flash of relief in his face was unexpected. It was also short-lived.

'That guy, Aidan, was the head honcho's son?'

She nodded. 'Worse. He was a jerk sober and a bigger one when he wasn't.'

Her admission earned a knowing smirk. 'So I recall from your folks' party, although you were *very* defensive of him back then.'

'Why, thank you *again*, Mr Talbot,' she said sweetly. 'How could I ever get along without you to constantly remind me of my mistakes?'

He ignored her sarcasm, determined to get the rest of the story from her as quickly as possible. There was something way too stressful about being in a bedroom with K.C..

'So tell me,' he said, moving rapidly from *that* disturbing train of thought. 'How long before the police were told about the letters?'

'I'm not sure.' Setting the brush aside, she turned to face him. 'Station security were informed straight away, but the first I knew of the police being involved was when my car got bombed.'

'Which was when?'

'Two days after we filmed the condom commercial.'

'But weren't you the only cast member to do that commercial?'

'Yes, but—'

'Then surely the cops could have figured out that—'

'Ryan,' she said, her hand automatically touching his arm, her tone reasoning, 'the ad hadn't even been edited at that stage, let alone gone to air. No one outside of a few industry people would have known I was in it.'

'And naturally everyone assumed the nut was an outsider.' He sent her a chilling look. 'Which today proves to have been a potentially fatal assumption.'

'Don't!' she said, pulling back. 'It's bad enough thinking *anyone* could want to kill me, much less someone I've worked with.'

'I'm sorry, honey, but it's a possibility you have to face.'

She shook her head. 'Uh-uh. I won't, *I can't* believe that.' Yet as she spoke the denial it left a taste of fear in her mouth. Again she shook her head, but the expression on Ryan's face told her that he wouldn't be swayed from his opinion. That more than anything terrified her; history showed that when she and Ryan held differing opinions hers was usually the wrong one.

'Oh, God...' She twisted her hair in agitation. 'What am I going to do? This is all getting too, too crazy.'

Finding himself fighting the urge to fold her into his arms and kiss her until her eyes were drowsy with pas-

sion instead of alert with fear, Ryan knew it was time
to get the hell out of there. *Fast.*

'We'll work something out, kiddo,' he said, taking the
safe option of shoving his hands into his pockets. 'But
since I think better on a full stomach, why don't you
order up some food from Room Service while I shower,
huh?'

Thirty minutes later, against a background of soft rock
courtesy of the hotel radio and with a bottle of
Chardonnay, they were seated at the suite's dining table
and trying to unwind. By mutual agreement the subject
of fires and stalkers was being temporarily kept on hold.

Kirrily hadn't had much enthusiasm for food, until
she'd seen it, which was why she'd only ordered one
shrimp salad and why she was pinching succulent
prawns from Ryan's plate as quickly as he could peel
them.

'Let me know when you're bloated, K.C., and I'll save
you the trouble of belching,' he teased as yet another
crustacean was plucked from his fingers and lifted towards her lips.

Her hand paused and she sent him an insulted look.
'My mother said ladies *never* belch.'

'Did she also say ladies never peel their own prawns?'

'No, but I've always found it's faster and less messy
to have someone else do it.'

'OK, so *you* peel some so I find out for myself.'

'Nope!' she said, swiping another two from the plate
before he had a chance. 'You'll just have to trust me on
this.' She grinned, oohing and ahing with delight after
she'd eaten one.

'Obviously you weren't paying attention to Claire's
etiquette lesson about how it's bad manners to take the
last piece of food.'

'Oh, quit grumbling,' Kirrily said, though his complaint had been laced with humour. 'You're the one who
said I should eat something.'

He laughed. 'And when have you *ever* done anything I suggested?'

'Lots of times. Besides—' The look of alarm on Ryan's face as he recoiled in his chair stopped her short. 'What?' she asked. 'What's the matter?'

'I'm waiting for lightning to strike the room.'

'Ooh! You...' the punch she aimed for his arm missed '...rat!'

'A hungry rat.' He greedily eyed the prawn she still held. 'If you aren't going to eat that thing, pass it this way; I'd like at least *two*.'

Watching him with malicious delight, she took a bite and sighed theatrically. A male grunt of disapproval ensued.

'Oh, here,' she said, nudging his lower lip with the remaining portion of moist pink meat. 'Never let it be said that Kirrily Cosgrove kept food from a starving man.'

Ryan lifted his eyes from the prawn being temptingly held to his mouth to the bright, laughing green eyes of the woman on his right. It ranked as one of the biggest mistakes he'd ever made; his heart slammed into his ribs with such violence that it seemed as if every internal organ he possessed vibrated from the force. In the wake of this, a need so strong that it was a physical pain swept through him, until he was conscious only of the hard, aching weight in his groin and the woman responsible for it. Mouth clamped shut, he swallowed hard, beseeching his brain to keep his body under control.

The suddenly rigid posture and expression of the man next to her alerted Kirrily that he'd ceased to be a willing participant in the light-hearted game. Indeed, beneath his fixed gaze, she felt she'd been cast as the aggressor in a battle that Ryan wanted no part of yet was determined to win. A tingle of excitement slid down her spine at the thought of defeating him by forcing his lips to take the fish against his will. Hot on the heels of that came the image of him nibbling her fingers right along with it. The notion left her almost breathless. It also energised her with recklessness.

'Well, c'mon,' she urged, continuing to brush the cool meat across his mouth. 'I can vouch it's good. Don't you want to taste the very last bit?'

Though Ryan managed a façade of immunity to her breathy cajoling, he could only take so much; ultimately it was her utterly feminine smile that sent the embryotic passion she'd sparked blazing out of control. She was offering prawns. He hungered for *her*. He grabbed her wrist as pent-up desire gave birth to anger!

'Stop it, K.C.!' Her hand, imprisoned in his, was forced to the table. 'Grow up!'

He stood so abruptly that his chair tipped back, and for an instant Kirrily was stunned speechless. Then her body started to do a slow burn, partly from anger but more from noting the pained expression on Ryan's face and the obvious bulge in his jeans before he turned away.

Ryan wanted her. Ryan Talbot wanted her as a woman! The thought made her giddy; knowing he hated himself for it made her angry. Watching the rise and fall of his shoulders as he stood with his back to her made her angrier still. Damn him! What was wrong with her?

'Is telling me to grow up a way of convincing yourself I'm still a child, Ryan, or an attempt to convince *me* I am?' The iciness in her tone surprised even Kirrily herself. She didn't feel cold.

'Because if it's the latter you're wasting your breath. And if it's the former then…' She paused, getting to her feet and moving until she stood less than a foot behind him. 'Well, Ryan, if it's the former, then the way you feel about prawns requires therapy.'

'If you know what's good for you, K.C.,' he said, his

voice and words strained, 'you'll shut the hell up and get out of this room, *now*.'

'Uh-uh, Ryan,' she said, dragging a trembling finger across his tense shoulders and down his spine. 'What's good for me is you...'

CHAPTER EIGHT

RYAN whirled round and grasped her forearms. 'What the hell do you want from me, K.C.?'

'The same thing you want from me.'

She took the small step needed to bring her flush against him and Ryan found himself torn between what his conscience told him to do and the dictates of his body.

'Of course,' she whispered, tracing the shell of his ear, then letting her fingers trail along his jaw and down to the thumping pulse in his throat, 'I *might* be wrong about what *you* want.' One eyebrow arched. 'Am I?'

He thought of a hundred reasons why he should release her and step away, but they crumbled a score at a time when challenged by her quick, short breaths and the feel of her womanly curves brushing against him. Over the years he'd experienced her attempts to play the innocent, the rebel, the wild child and, more lately, the independent career woman, but never before the seductress.

'Am I wrong, Ryan?'

He closed his eyes, feeling he was battling a thousand demons as she continued to press him, physically and verbally. Yes! he wanted to scream. Yes, dammit, you're wrong! But before he could verbalise the blatant lie her hand moved to seal his mouth and he found himself drowning in imploring light green eyes.

'You've never lied to me before, Ryan. Don't start now.'

Kirrily heard only his quick intake of breath before her body was bombarded from all directions with sensations of erotic bliss as her fingers were sucked between his lips and his hands cupped her buttocks to lift her against him. Instinctively her arms went around his neck and her legs embraced his hips.

'Tighter,' he muttered, his mouth suckling on the column of her throat. 'Hold me tighter.'

She obliged, nestling the dampening area between her thighs deeper into his hardness, the resulting male groan of approval filling her with feminine satisfaction. The movement of his mouth against her throat was hypnotic, but she was desperate for the taste of him, needing to feel again his tongue entwined with hers. Trusting her leg muscles and Ryan's strong, muscular arms to keep her from falling, she clutched at his head, forcing it back until his face was only centimetres from her own. Her heart lurched as his eyes, swimming with passion, fastened on hers; it was like viewing the intensity of her own desire, like looking at a mirror image of her own hunger.

'Ryan…kiss me…'

She was uncertain if the words were a command or a plea, but when her mouth was claimed with more brutality than she'd expected she viewed Ryan's aggression as a victory. He was responding to her as one highly aroused adult to another, without a shadow of protectiveness, and, drunk with the sensual power the notion unleashed, Kirrily matched her response to his. She grasped his hair as hard and as roughly as his fingers bit into her buttocks, she parried and duelled as greedily with his tongue as he did with hers and she nipped and laved his lips with the wanton abandon his identical actions provoked.

Ryan's mind was a kaleidoscope of emotions and sensations, all revolving around the woman in his arms—a woman more responsive than any he'd known, a woman whose passion was more infectious and potent than he'd ever imagined. The feel of her wrapped around him was both the sweetest and cruellest experience of his life. The flavour of her hot, honeyed mouth simultaneously fed his need yet left him hungering for more. He wanted this woman as he had no other.

Envisioning her naked and writhing beneath him as he buried himself deep inside her only intensified the ache in his groin. But the hungry male lust urging him to take her hard and fast was counteracted by a wave of tenderness.

This was K.C.! Even if it killed him he was going to take this slowly; she deserved better than wham bam thank you, ma'am! This was going to be the best damn sex she'd ever had and she was going to remember it for the rest of her life. But, all but scorched by the heat emanating from the woman in his arms, Ryan's good intentions went the way of water in hell the moment her hips started mimicking the suggestive thrusts of his tongue.

Kirrily didn't know how they managed to get from the dining room, but as Ryan tumbled them onto the mattress she didn't care.

'Condoms?'

The one word query was whispered between hot, wet kisses that effectively retarded Kirrily's comprehension skills. Trying to think while his hot male tongue was doing delicious things to her ear wasn't easy. 'Huh?' she mumbled as a shiver of desire shook her.

'Protection…have you got some?'

'Uh…um. My cosmetic bag… In my…suitcase.'

Long moments later she glimpsed a grateful smile as Ryan rolled off the bed, but being deprived of his body, even for the few seconds it took him to locate what he was after, had Kirrily's stomach tightening in dread; what if he had second thoughts, changed his mind…?

He didn't. Flipping the foil packets onto the nightstand, he resumed his position beside her and she moved into his arms with heartfelt relief, responding to his ardent mouth with all the warmth and wonder he alone created within her.

The touch of his hands against her skin as they lifted the hem of her sweatshirt sent the flames that his kisses had ignited raging out of control and the urgent need to feel those hands against her tight, throbbing nipples had her quickly taking over the task of disposing of her top. With want and need blurring into one, she started to lower her sweatpants, but stronger male hands stopped her.

Puzzled, she lifted her eyes to Ryan. 'What's…?'

His expression as he stared at her bared breasts was one of such complete reverence that it took her breath away. For Kirrily time was suspended as he tentatively moved forward to kiss each erect peak; when it started again she was nude and pinned beneath the glorious weight of an equally naked male whose hands were as eagerly inquisitive as her own.

Go slow. Go slow. Go slow. Ryan's mental chant was futile against the searing heat and velvet softness of the woman entwined with him. His mouth and hands couldn't get enough of her delicate feminine softness and her exploring fingers were driving him to the point of madness as they travelled the ridges and contours of his body. Fearing he'd explode before he brought her to fulfilment, he snagged her wrists, stretching her arms above her head. Startled, she let out a breathy little gasp, her taut, firm breasts lifting provocatively as she struggled for air.

When Ryan rose to his knees and straddled her, Kirrily's already manic heart pumped faster as she choked on a dozen different emotions. 'Ry-an…I want—'

'Shh, don't talk, just feel.'

'I…can't. You've…you've got my hands…'

A purely male smirk lit his face. 'Trust me, you aren't going to need them. Besides, either I take control now, honey, or we both get short-changed.'

He transferred his grip so that he had one hand free which he used to draw a seductive line down her throat, between her breasts and onward to the dark curls atop her thighs, causing her hips to jerk.

'You like that, huh?' His fingers travelled to her damp centre and teased her until she reproduced the action, in unison with a sucked-in gasp. Almost drowning in her responsiveness, he watched her face as his thumb skimmed the nub of her desire and one finger slipped into her. 'And it gets…better,' he vowed, his voice breaking at the feel of her wet readiness. 'Ah, Kirrily, we know it gets a hell of a lot better!'

Kirrily was unable to garner sufficient control over either her mind or vocal cords to make comment as his sensual and intimate caress continued. Her arousal intensified with each slow, taunting stroke, until it became almost a pleasurable pain that had her hips arching from the bed in pursuit of his hand at the slightest hint of its withdrawal.

Watching her lithe young body buck and squirm in response to his touch had Ryan gritting his teeth in an effort to hold himself in check. 'Easy, honey,' he whispered as she started tossing her head from side to side and struggling to free her hands. 'Relax…let it happen.'

His voice sounded as if it came from another dimension as it drifted through the rainbow of lights exploding in Kirrily's mind, body and soul. She tried to tell him what she was seeing and hearing, but suddenly she was engulfed by sensation so radiant that it was all she could manage to cry out his name…

Though Ryan released her hands when the orgasmic quakes electrifying her body threatened his own, having her melt in his hand equated with witnessing an atomic explosion; he was a victim before the fallout had even reached him, and opening the condom became the slowest, most complex task he'd ever undertaken. Holding his breath, he fumbled to sheath himself with trembling fingers.

'Ry-Ryan.' Her voice was as soft as an angel's. 'Let me.'

The awed expression on her face combined with the tentative hand on his wrist almost made him fall apart. The emotion erupting within him was a strange cocktail of tenderness, desire and an anticipation that bordered on fear. If he hadn't waited all his life for this moment, then it felt as if he had and he wasn't going to blow it prematurely. He shook his head, more at his appalling pun than a response to her offer, but by then the task was completed.

Bracing himself on his arms above her, he closed his eyes in the hope of slowing himself down, but it was a losing battle the second her hands moved over his buttocks and she arched her hips into his.

'Show me "better", Ryan,' she said. *'Now.'*

Her eagerness sent his lust into overdrive and his last thought as he drove into her slick warmth was that at least he'd brought her to completion first...

Aware of the mattress moving beneath her, Kirrily opened her eyes. There was sufficient light streaming from the dining area for her to follow Ryan's naked progress to the bathroom, but she cursed the dimness of the room for robbing her of the chance to study the movement of his taut-to-the-touch butt in more detail. A tiny moan escaped from her at the recollection of the contrast between the soft skin of his buttocks and the hair-roughened toughness of his chest, yet she'd loved touching every millimetre of his male flesh. Nor did she have any complaints about the way he'd touched hers! Kirrily knew she was grinning like a half-dazed idiot but didn't care! *Nothing* had ever felt so right, so *wonderful*!

Nothing could have prepared her for the unimaginable pleasures that Ryan had shown her or the ethereal bliss now cocooning her. It was as if she'd had a spell cast upon her—for half a heartbeat she worried that she might only have dreamt the most spectacular event of her life; then Ryan reappeared at the door of the bathroom and she knew that reality had its own magic.

With nothing but a towel draped around his hips and his hair tousled from their passion, he looked so blatantly male and sexy that it took Kirrily's hormone-drugged brain a moment to register that for some reason he also looked—

'You...you...!' Fury coloured his face as he strode to the foot of the bed keeping a white-knuckled grip on the towel. 'Why the bloody hell didn't you tell me you were a *virgin*?'

'I...I—'

'*What?*' he sneered, with a venom that made her flinch. 'Wanted to see if your seductress act worked as well in real life as it does on television?' In one motion he picked up her sweatshirt and threw it, hitting her in the chest. 'Well, guess what—it *does*! Congratulations!'

Stunned, Kirrily could only clutch the clothing to her bareness. 'Ryan...' she started, only to find her voice barely audible. 'Ryan...I don't know why you're so upset. It's no—'

His cold, mirthless laugh cracked the air, vaporising her good feelings and replacing them with confusion and shame. She gave up trying to read the emotion behind his eyes because her own were beginning to fill with tears.

'*Upset?*' He shook his head. 'I'm not upset, K.C., I'm way beyond that. Do you have any idea how *disgusted* I'm feeling right now?'

That soft but obvious insult belatedly activated what vestige of pride Kirrily still possessed. 'You're disgusted?' she snapped, praying she was a good enough actress to portray anger when pain was crippling her. 'Well, if *this* is typical of post-coital bliss, sex is gonna be a one-off experience for this little black duck! Get out of my room, Ryan Talbot!'

When he didn't move, she hurled a pillow at him.

He deflected it with ease. 'K.C., hang on—'

'Get out and stay out!' she screeched, launching a second pillow. 'Outta my room *and* my life!'

For a moment it looked as if he was going to ignore her command, but as her hand closed around the bedside radio he changed his mind.

Ryan emerged from his room at seven the next morning to find Kirrily on the phone. In an abstract way he noted her jeans and bomber jacket, though his mind was picturing her as she'd been in his arms last night; her hair flowing in a smooth curtain down her back made his fingers twitch with the temptation to feel its silkiness again.

'And I'd appreciate it if you could order me a cab... Yes. Thank you, forty minutes will be fine.'

'Fine for what?' he asked as she disconnected the call.

She pivoted towards him, her face revealing surprise and the dark smudges of a sleepless night, yet a second later her chin lifted to a defiant angle.

'I'm leaving this morning.'

'I know.' He moved to the courtesy beverage counter. 'We're booked on a flight back to Sydney at ten-fifteen.'

'Uh-uh. You can go to hell for all I care, but you'll go on your own, Ryan Talbot. I'm staying in Melbourne. I'd sooner die than suffer your company ever again.'

'Be careful what you wish for, K.C.,' he warned, and saw instant regret for her choice of words dim her features.

'If wishes counted for anything I'd have woken up this morning and discovered everything that's happened in the past two days has been nothing more than a nightmare.' Her eyes narrowed as she looked at him and Ryan knew she wasn't talking about the fire. 'The sooner you're out of my face and hundreds of miles away, the happier I'll be. Stalker or no stalker.'

'I've no intention of letting you stay here alone. You can hate me as much as you like, but don't be so immature as to think I'll allow you to put yourself in jeopardy for the sake of your pride.'

'Right! Like you'd give a damn about *my* pride after the demolition job you did on it last night.'

'K.C., I—'

'No!' She held her hand up like a policeman stopping traffic. 'The last thing I want from you is an apology.'

'Really? Well, that's good,' he replied. 'Because I'm not giving you one; the way I see it, if anyone deserves an apology for last night it's *me*.'

Shock made her gasp. '*You? For what?*'

'For having the responsibility of taking your virginity foisted onto me, that's what! You set me up, K.C..'

'*Foisted? Taking* my virginity?' A disbelieving laugh broke from her. 'How did I *set you up*, for God's sake?'

'You deliberately came on to me and responded like you were an old hand at seduction. Hell! Taking advantage of you after I'd spent years trying to protect you from hormone-driven scumbags would've been enough to face, but discovering *I'm* the only scumbag who's ever touched you... Sheesh! That's—'

'The greatest load of *rubbish* I've ever heard!' she burst out. 'For a start you didn't *take* my virginity—I *gave* it to you—'

'Great, rub it right in—'

'In the second place, the only reason I *was* still a virgin is because when I was a teenager and practically breaking my neck to rid myself of the stigma of virginity *you*, Ryan Talbot, scared away every candidate I lined up! You even gave me a brotherly lecture on how losing one's virginity was something that should simply happen, without conscious decision, when the time was right.

'Well, guess what?' she went on, hands on her hips. 'Last night without any conscious decision to *set you up* the timing was right. If I came across as experienced maybe it's because I've had professional direction in love scenes. Maybe it's because reading articles like "What Makes Sex Great" or "Being Brilliant Between the Sheets" and so forth in women's magazines provided me with enough theory on the subject to stop me from coming across as a sexual klutz! Or maybe...*and I suspect this is what really scares the stuffing out of you*,' she said, sending him a smug look, 'it's because the chemistry between us was so strong my instincts just kicked into overdrive all by themselves.'

He simply stood and stared at her, his face tense, his stance rigid.

'Well, like it or not, *that's* what happened,' she said, when he volunteered no response. 'Call it chemistry, physical attraction or just plain old lust, but the fact is *I* didn't consider my virginity one way or the other. You, on the other hand, obviously *assumed* it was long gone, otherwise you wouldn't be so ticked off at finding it wasn't! *Your* mistake, not mine. So don't try and haul me along on your guilt trip. And, furthermore, it's about time you put your promise to Steve to take care of me into perspective.'

A twitch of a muscle near the side of his mouth was Kirrily's only hint that she'd finally managed to penetrate his statue-like indifference. Feeling satisfied, she snatched a much needed breath before continuing.

'Take credit for protecting me from "hormone-driven scumbags" in the past if you want, but don't make the mistake of thinking you can be responsible for *my* hormones or any other part of my life *now*. I'm twenty-four years old, Ryan, *three years older* than my brother was when he died and three years older than you were when you assumed responsibility for me. So, as of now, I'm absolving you of your role as guardian angel over me.'

Though emotionally drained, Kirrily forced herself not to bolt from the room—not only because she knew Ryan would expect her to make a dramatic exit, but because she felt their entire future relationship depended on her facing whatever rebuttals he fired. Still, the weight of the lengthening silence, his inscrutable expression and penetrating gaze made her feel almost claustrophobic.

'What,' he said finally, 'if I don't want to be absolved of it?'

'As you've told me more than once, "What we want and what we get isn't always within our control."'

His mouth twisted wryly. 'Is that another reference to last night?'

'No…no,' she said, genuinely puzzled, but not willing to let herself be sidetracked. 'Look, I know you've only ever had my best interests at heart, Ryan—' she ignored his sardonic laugh '—but I'm an adult now. I don't need a keeper.'

'So prove it,' he challenged her. 'Cancel the cab and agree to fly back to Sydney with me.'

'Under the circumstances I don't think that would be a smart thing to do.'

'Oh, get real, K.C.!' Impatience and disbelief coloured his face. 'The circumstances are that some nut is trying to kill you! What happened between us doesn't rank as an issue compared to that.'

'Ryan, I—'

'If you want a promise that I won't lay a hand on you, then fine, you've got it!' he said, closing the distance between them and making an instant liar of himself by taking hold of her shoulders. 'But hell, Kirrily, surely you can't think you'll be safer with a maniac than with me?'

Her mind baulked at his use of her full name. She thought she'd imagined that he'd called her Kirrily while making love to her, but perhaps she hadn't and, if not, it raised an interesting question. Of course she might be reading too much into it, but could his sudden use of her full name after fifteen years mean he was, subconsciously at least, seeing her in a mature light?

Until now she'd never considered that Ryan's exclusive use of Steven's nickname for her might be a way of reinforcing the brotherly relationship he'd assumed with her. Yet, in hindsight, the way his passion had switched to anger after discovering she'd been a virgin seemed to indicate he was torn between acknowledging her as a consenting adult and an innocent he was responsible for protecting.

From her perspective there was no denying that around Ryan she'd always felt safe. *Too* safe. It was as if she were an expensive piece of porcelain he felt should be kept locked in the china cabinet so no disaster could befall her. On one level his protectiveness was touching and reassuring, on another it was infuriating, but Kirrily now realised that emotionally there'd never been a time when she'd been immune to Ryan. And she never would be, not after experiencing the raw energy and intensity of his lovemaking.

Even now she could feel the heat of his hands through the thickness of her jacket. His touch and nearness were more than enough to unfurl ribbons of desire within her, and the sensation deafened her to his, no doubt, pragmatic argument about returning to Sydney. She could only watch in silent fascination as his mouth switched from tight-lipped irritation to the deliberately slow actions of enunciation to bursts of rapid speech revealing glimpses of teeth and tongue. To an observer she probably looked like someone who depended on lip-reading, but the trouble was that she didn't want to read those lips, she wanted to *feel* them—feel them all the way from the tip of her head to the soles of her feet.

'Damn it, K.C.!' His voice rose enough to penetrate

her thoughts. 'You haven't heard a word I've said, have you?'

It was impossible to stifle a grin. 'No,' she replied honestly. 'But I'll happily agree with you and go back to Sydney if you want.'

'Happily agree with me? That'll be the day!' As he surveyed her, a suspicious gleam entered his eye and he stepped away from her. 'What's going on in that complex mind of yours?'

'Nothing. But you're right. I'm safer in Sydney with you than on my own down here.'

'Well, I'll be damned,' he said, looking smug. 'After years of denial you're admitting you need me to protect you?'

'Yes, Ryan,' she said without reservation. 'I need you.' Nothing in his expression hinted that he'd noticed her deliberate avoidance of the the word 'protection', but, afraid she'd perhaps revealed too much, she hurried on. 'I mean there's no way whoever's stalking me would expect to find me living in Cabarita and working for a building-supply firm.' She grinned. 'I doubt the cops could have come up with a better idea if I was a candidate for witness protection.'

A wavelet of unease rippled through Ryan's gut. 'How many people did you tell you were going to Sydney?'

'Apart from my agent, Carole, just my flatmates and friends.'

'Who?' he pressed. 'Who *exactly* have you given my address to?'

'I dunno.' She shrugged as if the question were irrelevant. 'Anyway, I gave out your phone number, not the address.'

Ryan turned away as she started to rattle off various names. The knowledge that she'd practically advertised her previous trip to Sydney bothered him. It bothered him a lot...

CHAPTER NINE

RYAN was relieved when they finally arrived back at Mascot Airport around one o'clock on Sunday afternoon—not just because being in Sydney put added distance between K.C. and the lunatic harassing her, but because the Jag was still where he'd left it.

Given the recent spate of warnings by police and insurance companies, leaving the car overnight in the public car park had seemed a blatant invitation to car thieves. But yesterday, by the time he'd made the necessary flight and hotel arrangements, packed, then run the wayward Major to ground and deposited him into Mrs Dunford's care, he'd been reluctant to rely on a cab getting them to the airport in time to catch their plane. Actually, considering the way he'd flaunted the speed limit driving there, the fact he'd avoided both the highway patrol *and* car thieves was nothing short of miraculous.

If his luck held he'd have no trouble getting K.C. to go along with the idea which had sprung into his head on the flight back to Sydney. *Sure*—like he'd get *two* miracles in twenty-four hours!

Disarming the car alarm, he opened the passenger door for K.C.. 'I want to make a slight detour on the way home,' he said casually.

'OK, but could you get my cellular phone out of my bag before you put it in the boot? I want to make some calls.'

He obliged without comment and she was busy

punching out telephone numbers when he slid behind the steering wheel.

Ryan found mobile phones an intrusion which, had he not needed one for business, he could cheerfully have lived without; K.C. regarded them as one of life's top three necessities along with food and water. Since he wasn't sure how far he'd get before she stopped buying the 'slight detour' story, he hoped the phone would distract her until jumping from a moving Jag wasn't an option she'd take.

While convincing her to return to Sydney had been achieved with minimum debate, Ryan wasn't counting on two easy victories over her stubbornness in one lifetime, much less one day. He might like to believe common sense would continue to keep her agreeable to his taking control of the situation, but at best K.C. only greeted common sense with grudging resignation; she'd equate the passive surrender of her independence a second time with death.

Acid bile rose in his throat as his subconscious again highlighted the gravity of the situation. His eyes darted to the woman seated beside him. Like it or lump it, even if it meant she hated him till his dying day, he was going to do whatever was necessary to protect her.

An hour later K.C. was still chatting away on her cellular phone to her agent as if innocently unaware of where they were. Ryan knew otherwise; he'd seen her frown twice as they passed signposts indicating their route. So why wasn't she questioning this 'slight detour' that so far had taken them nearly a hundred kilometres out of their way, huh?

Why was she sending him benign smiles in between a string of phone calls that had to run into a four-figure bill and treating him to such perfect politeness that they could have passed for strangers? Ryan didn't like it...not one damn bit!

He continued questioning K.C.'s curious malleability,

but, devoid of an explanation, determinedly diverted his attention away from his beautiful but enigmatic passenger. It worked for about three seconds, then the soft, melodious tone of her laughing at something her agent said jarred him to the point where he wanted to snatch the phone from her. Knowing the urge was an immature need to take revenge for the effect she was having on him, he gripped the steering wheel tightly enough to cut off all blood circulation to his fingers.

It wasn't natural to be this close to K.C. and not have her breathy, excited chatter directed at him. Hell, he'd rather have her arguing with him than ignoring him! Maybe, he reasoned, avoiding conversation with him was her way of dealing with what had happened last night. If so, he hoped it was working for her because it sure wasn't helping him any! God, he'd never been so aware of a woman in his entire life! If anything, making love to her last night had fed his attraction, not cured it, and, despite his promise, keeping his hands off her was going to be the hardest thing he'd ever have to do.

He cast a furtive glance at her, then recognised it for the foolish move it was the instant his eyes collided with her vivid green ones; the physical impact of her shy blush had him clamping his teeth together and visualising a cold—*very* cold—shower.

By the time she ended her call he felt as if every nerve in his body was tied in knots.

'So what did your agent have to say?' he asked, in what he hoped was a casual voice. 'Any big Hollywood offers?'

'I should be so lucky. All she's got is a walk-on role in a sitcom which calls for me to wear a purple wig and say two lines. I passed on it.'

'Why?'

A heavy sigh carried from the passenger seat. 'The show's in its death throes; it's hardly going to resurrect my career.'

Complete silence ensued between them for several kilometres until another signpost came into view. When Kirrily again noted it without making comment it forced Ryan to speak.

'Aren't you going to ask me where we're going?'

'Nope. I figured that out a while back.'

'Oh?'

'Yeah, though it's hardly what I'd call a *slight detour.* We're going to Bowral; Mum mentioned you bought a block of land there.' She twisted in her seat so she was facing him. 'Am I right?'

He shot her a quick glance and was irrationally pleased to see a smile on her face. He reverted his eyes to the road, wondering if he'd ever before been as pre-occupied with Kirrily's happiness as he was now.

'Well?' she prompted. 'Am I right or not?'

'Half-right.'

'So what's the other half?'

'If I tell you it won't be a surprise.'

'If you don't tell me, I'm out of this car at the next set of traffic lights.'

It was an empty threat since there were no lights on the expressway, but the return of her dry tone sounded like music to his ears and he couldn't resist baiting her some more.

'Where's all that polite civility and blind obedience you've been treating me to since reading me the Riot Act this morning?'

'All good things in moderation, Ryan,' she quipped. 'Now, are you going to tell me what this surprise is or not?'

'Not.'

'*Ryan!* I demand to know why you're taking me to Bowral!'

He grinned. 'Ah! Now there's the K.C. we all know and love—bossy, temperamental, stubborn…'

Whatever other less than endearing terms he assigned

to her, Kirrily didn't hear because the word 'love' was echoing loudly in her brain. Though she knew that without 'in' preceding it coming from Ryan it probably meant no more than it did coming from her parents or any other relative. Trevor Nichols might think Ryan was in love with her, but with a disastrous marriage to his name Trev's credibility in matters of the heart wasn't exactly iron-clad.

Yet, regardless of how Ryan felt, after last night Kirrily knew she was as deeply in love as she was ever going to get. It didn't matter that she had no previous lovers by which to measure her reaction to Ryan; she *knew* without a shadow of doubt that she'd never feel this way about another man. She'd been born to love Ryan and she'd die loving only him. The question was what to do about it.

With any other man she'd have pursued him with an 'I've got nothing to lose' attitude, yet with Ryan she sensed she might lose everything. Then again, considering she'd already surrendered her heart, virginity and a sizeable chunk of her pride to him, there wasn't much left to risk!

Except your independence, an inner voice reminded her.

Yes, she conceded on a mental sigh, *that* was what made her reluctant to follow her heart—the fear that Ryan's love would be too all-consuming. To Kirrily, who preferred to act on impulse rather than give self-doubt time to overpower her, Ryan Talbot was so damned sure of himself that she was scared his confidence would undermine her independence. What if, after winning the only man she wanted in her life, he became the only thing in her life? Steven had held that status in Jayne's life even from beyond the grave. The thought of being that emotionally bound to another person terrified Kirrily.

She shivered as a renegade thought burst into her

brain; supposing she ignored the threat to her identity, be it real or imagined, and pursued Ryan? Wouldn't she be risking their complex but long-standing friendship? Friends could become lovers, but could lovers go back to being friends? While Kirrily wanted to be much more than friends with Ryan, she wasn't sure if she could live with being anything less...

'Hey, K.C.!' The exuberant address pulled her from her introspection. 'If you keep frowning like that you'll get premature wrinkles, and then where will your career be?'

'I hate to think, since it's in the toilet now.'

It was his turn to frown. 'Things are *that* bad?'

'Let's see... I've been sacked from a successful, long-running series on the premise that I'm difficult to work with,' she said, holding up her thumb. 'I'm being chased by a maniac who wants me dead.' Up went a finger. 'My home, which I'm struggling to make payments on since I'm unemployed, has been reduced to a pile of ash, my agent has nothing suitable for me on the horizon, and I'm totally unskilled for another career.' She held her now open hand where he could see it. 'That's five counts against me, Ryan. Previously the most I've ever had at any one time was three. So, yeah,' she said, 'I'd say things are *that* bad.'

Catching her off guard, Ryan snared her raised hand and brought it to rest on his thigh. Slowly he spread her fingers wide by inserting his own between them. Kirrily found the action mind-numbingly erotic and had to fight the temptation to explore the firm muscle she felt beneath the worn denim of his jeans.

'First,' he said, his eyes on the road, 'the way I hear it you weren't sacked; your contract wasn't renewed because you placed too high a value on yourself. Their loss, not yours.' The look he gave her as he curled her thumb into her palm made her heart flip.

'Secondly,' he continued, his eyes reverting to the

windscreen, 'the police have made catching the guy has-
sling you a top priority now. And he's not likely to be
able to trace you since no one knows exactly where you
are except me, and I'm not going to let *anything* happen
to you. Understand?'

The intensity of his gaze and the total confidence in
his voice reassured her as nothing else could have. Not
trusting her vocal cords, she merely nodded.

'Good.' He gave her hand a gentle squeeze before
curling down the second of her fingers. 'Now, your
house was insured, right?'

'Y-y-y-yes.'

'Well, then, financially you're not in such dire
straights. In case you've forgotten, you have *excellent*
connections in the building game; between our dads and
me, rebuilding your house isn't going to be a hardship.'
Her middle finger was turned down. 'And you *aren't*
unemployed,' he stressed. 'You're what's commonly
known in the acting profession as "between projects",
only, instead of waiting tables or driving cabs, you're
working in the accounts department of Talbot's Building
Supplies.'

As her ring finger received identical treatment to the
others he directed a hundred-megawatt smile at her that
Kirrily was sure had done major damage to her heart if
not actually melted it. 'Wh…what about this problem?'
she asked, jiggling her still outstretched little finger; beneath it she felt his thigh muscle contract.

'You mean being unskilled? Not an issue,' he whispered in response to her nod, enclosing her fist in his
much larger one before lifting it to his mouth and placing
the softest of kisses against her inner wrist. 'You'll suc-
ceed at anything you put your heart and mind to, Kirrily.
I know from experience you're a very quick study.'

She didn't kid herself that he was talking about how
she'd handled the invoices at the office. Yet before she
could formulate a reply her hand was back in her lap,

and all she knew was that Bruce Springsteen was blasting from the car's state-of-the-art CD player, a road sign was advising the exit for the Southern Tablelands town of Bowral and that Ryan had not only called her Kirrily again but he'd kissed her without any prompting on her part. In an effort to compose herself, she stared out at the gently rolling hills of the Southern Tablelands.

As a child she'd spent many a Sunday afternoon with her parents combing the antiques and craft stores in the towns of Bowral, Mittagong, Moss Vale and Kangaroo Valley and the beauty and tranquillity of the area had always appealed to her. Yet residency in the area didn't come cheap, and what had once merely been a small rural community had become a fashionable area for assorted celebrities and politicians if only on a part-time basis. Large, elegant homes were sited on manicured, multi-acre blocks, some viewable from the road by virtue of their hilltop locations, others screened for privacy by high concrete walls with built-in security systems.

'Not exactly a first-home-buyers' neighbourhood,' she noted as she saw a chauffeur-driven limo waiting at iron gates which, from road level, revealed a long gravelled drive and nothing else.

Ryan told her the property belonged to a retired titled politician whose source of wealth had always been under scrutiny.

'If he's one of your neighbours, Ryan, I'm not sure if I should be impressed by your success or disappointed that you've outgrown your blue-collar roots. Still, as an investment you've got it made.'

'What makes you think I bought here only as an investment?'

'Well, it wouldn't be practical for you to *live* here. What with the hours you put in at the office, the commuting would kill you. Besides, the night-life would be next to non-existent.'

He sent her a questioning look. 'Contrary to what you

imagine, my wild night-life is usually restricted to business dinners.'

'Yeah, right. And you picked up that blonde bimbo you brought to Christmas dinner at a builders' convention.'

'As it happens, *Rachel* happens to be the state accounts manager for a major firm; she hardly qualifies as a bimbo.'

'*Hardly* qualifies, *almost* qualifies, *definitely* qualifies…' K.C. shrugged. 'The point is you *didn't* pick her up at a business dinner.'

'True. *She* picked *me* up at a trade seminar. She works for a major structural erection firm.'

'I'll just bet she does,' Kirrily mumbled, not intending her words to be heard, but, like everything else about him, Ryan's hearing was perfect.

'You're jealous!' he accused her, clearly amused by the notion.

'I am not!'

'No?'

'*No!*' She scrambled to save what little dignity she had left. 'I've never in my life wanted to be an accounts manager, state or otherwise.'

'Does that mean you won't miss working at Talbot's?'

She frowned. 'Is that a backhanded way of firing me or something?'

He tossed her only the quickest of looks as he turned onto an untarred road. 'Is there a reason I *should* fire you?'

Kirrily thought of the way she'd spent Friday bringing the invoices up to date. 'Not any more,' she said drily. There was no way she was going to respond to the questioning eyebrow he raised at her words.

'Close your eyes.'

His words threw her. 'What?'

'Close your eyes,' he repeated.

'Why?'

'Humour me.'

She sighed. 'OK, they're shut. But I'd like to point out that I wasn't put on this earth solely to humour *you*, Ryan Talbot. I think I've already gone above and beyond the call of graciousness in my acceptance of this "slight detour", as you—'

'Close the mouth and open the lids, K.C.'

The retort to his amused tone died as her eyes fixed on the sight before her. The Colonial-styled home with its sweeping sandstone veranda took her breath away. Her glance swung between it and Ryan twice before she spoke.

'Oh, my... It's gorgeous. It's... Who owns it?'

'Me.'

'*You!* You mean you bought it?'

'Nope, built it.'

'But...I thought you'd only bought a block of land.'

'I did. Well, ten acres actually,' he qualified. 'Then I put a house on it.'

She ignored his glib grin simply because she was so overawed. 'And what a house.'

'You like it, huh?'

'Are you kidding? It's wonderful! It's...it's better than wonderful... Dad was right—you *are* one hell of an architect!'

'What?' He looked offended. 'You mean he didn't say I was a hell of a bricklayer, carpenter, plumber—'

'You really *built* this by yourself? No contractors?'

'Pretty much. Though in the interests of self-preservation I had someone else do the electrical wiring.'

'Wise move,' she said. 'Especially for someone who once blacked out the entire block trying to modify the lights on your house one Christmas.'

'Give me a break,' he groaned. 'I was sixteen. How was I to know there was already an overload on supply due to the electrical storm? Besides, you wouldn't even remember it; you were what...*four*?'

His defensive tone made her chuckle. 'True, but the story has practically become a legend. When I was in primary school they used it as an example in 'don't let this happen to you' safety talks.'

'Very funny. Here.' He removed the keys from the ignition and handed them to her. 'Go open up while I get out our stuff.'

'Our stuff?' Her eyes darkened with confusion. 'Why?'

'Because,' he responded, braced for the argument he knew he was inviting, 'we're staying here until the police get the guy who's harassing you.'

'*What?* Ryan, that could take *ages*—'

'Maybe, but I'm not going to let you try and handle this on your own. So either you agree to stay here with me or...'

'Or what?'

'I call Claire and Jack and tell them what's going on.'

'You will *not!*' she said. 'I don't want Mum and Dad worried.'

'Fair enough, but either you agree to stay here or I'm calling them.' Her lips parted in a way that preceded speech, but Ryan beat her to it. 'Save your arguments, K.C. There's no way I'm giving in on this so you might as well accept that, like it or not.'

'Are you through playing God?'

'Look, I know you think you can handle anything life throws at you on your own, and maybe in normal circumstances you can—'

'Gee, thanks for that generous vote of confidence,' she muttered, turning away.

'Ah, hell, K.C.,' he said, thumping the steering wheel. 'You can't deny this whole deal is way beyond normal for *anyone*. You heard what that cop said yesterday— you've become the victim of violent crime and need to take certain precautions.'

'So it was the police who suggested I hide out here?'

'Well, no…that was my idea. But once you stop being stubborn and thinking total independence is the ultimate virtue you'll realise staying here with me is the best option you've got. *In fact*,' he said firmly, deciding he'd soft-pedalled for long enough, 'it's the *only* option you've got.'

'I agree with you,' Kirrily said, getting out of the car.

'You agree with me?' Shock rendered him incapable of moving. *'Again?'*

She nodded. 'Guess I'm getting pretty good at discarding unnecessary virtues, huh?'

Watching her bound up the steps of the house, Ryan decided either someone had slipped something into his coffee on the plane and he was hallucinating, or someone had slipped something into K.C.'s—in which case he wanted a lifetime supply of it!

CHAPTER TEN

THE memory of her own, charred little house still fresh, sadness squeezed Kirrily's heart as she slipped the key into the shiny brass lock; yet she was also aware of a tingling excitement at the prospect of exploring a house designed and built entirely from the mind of the man she loved. Her heart gave a funny little skip.

The daughter of a tradesman, she appreciated the expert carpentry which allowed the heavy double doors to glide open with the minimum of effort. Knowing Ryan wouldn't settle for anything less than perfection, she didn't expect the majestic beauty of the house to cease with its exterior, but still she was awed by the craftsmanship that greeted her entrance.

The floor, a mosaic of Federation tiles with an intricate design of cream, deep green and burnt reds, was a delicate complement to the strength of the Jarrah woodwork and avocado walls. Kirrily calculated the floor area at about twelve by thirty-five feet, but, regardless of its length, it was too imposing to be called a mere hallway. At the far end were large double doors identical to those on her immediate left and right; further along, two single though equally solid doors faced each other. All were intricately carved and closed; curiosity begged her to open one.

'Now I know how contestants on game shows feel,' she muttered, and heard Ryan laugh behind her.

She turned, but before she had a chance to say anything a high-pitched wail broke the air. A scream burst from her as she clamped her hands to her ears. Dropping the bags, Ryan hurried past her to open the single right-hand-side door. Within moments silence was restored, but her much tested nerves still vibrated.

'Sorry. I forgot I'd shortened the activating time when I set it last.' Ryan's explanation did little to calm her, especially since there was more amusement than sincerity in his eyes. 'You've got to admit it's a pretty effective deterrent,' he said.

Kirrily wanted to throttle him; instead she made a show of glancing around the unfurnished foyer. 'I assume, since the alarm works, the complete absence of furniture is some kind of extreme example of minimalistic decorating.'

'Nah,' he said, moving back to close the front door. 'It's the result of a guy who doesn't have time to shop for furniture.'

'So why not hire a decorator?'

'Because I want someone who'll *ask* then try and understand what *I* want, not somebody who thinks they already *know* what I want.'

'And what's that?'

He frowned. 'A style that suits me *and* the house.'

'Sort of late nineteenth-century and arrogantly commanding, huh?' Ignoring his droll look, she turned in a slow circle, again surveying the surroundings. 'Well, if *I* was decorating this room,' she said, 'I'd scour the local antique stores for one of those big old hall stands; you know with hat hooks and an umbrella stand. *Not* a reproduction,' she stressed. 'Something that's got the personality and scars of time. And I'd hang dozens of old sepia photos of pioneers and family ancestors.'

'I don't have any,' he said.

'Oh, they don't necessarily have to be *your* ancestors,' she dismissed airily. 'Anyone's will do.'

Ryan stayed silent as she continued to roam around,

at times frowning in concentration, at others caressing the timberwork as if it were a living thing.

'Maybe a mirror,' she muttered, in a way that suggested she was talking more to herself than to him now. Her eyes were narrowed, as if she was visualising the room as she spoke. 'And something along the lines of a fountain—'

'A *fountain*?' Ryan practically gasped. Only K.C. would entertain the notion of putting a naked cupid spouting water in—

'Don't be ridiculous!' she said, as if reading his mind. 'I was going to say a fountain-*like* centrepiece, to close things down a bit. You know—so you don't get the feeling you're standing in an empty parking lot? Perhaps a huge urn,' she mused with a frown. 'Something say about shoulder-height, but *interesting*, not garish.'

'You surprise yet again, K.C.,' he said. 'I'd have thought your tastes would've run along more—'

'Outrageously theatrical lines?' she supplied, turning to him.

He shrugged. 'Like I said, you're full of surprises.' The thing was, he mused, some surprises he could deal with calmly and rationally and some he couldn't...like last night.

Kirrily found herself unable to look away from the soul-searching gaze he directed at her. At first she told herself that the reason she felt as if they were the only people on earth was due to the room's emptiness and isolated rural silence, but her body quickly reminded her she'd felt the exact same way in an elegantly furnished hotel amid Melbourne's dense city noise.

No...it wasn't exactly the same. The feelings his look sparked in her now were slightly different—more subtle. His actions and eyes last night had scrambled her body so crazily that she'd felt she'd have exploded had he not satisfied her, whereas now...now her heart-rate had become so languorous that she feared it would stop altogether. For it wasn't solely passion or desire shining from his half-hooded eyes but something else too—something she wanted so badly she wasn't game to put a name to it.

'C'mon,' he said roughly, shattering the atmosphere. 'I'll give you the fifty-cent tour. This has been so fascinating I can't wait to get your expert advice on what else the house needs.'

His tone put Kirrily on the defensive. 'Forget it,' she said tersely. 'I'd just as soon look round on my own if you're going to patronise me. I'd hardly expect you to approve of *anything* I did. And what's more I never claimed to be an expert in interior design; my suggestions were purely instinctive.'

That's the problem, Ryan thought; lately everything about K.C. seemed suggestive and came down to instincts—very basic carnal instincts! Hell, he didn't need this much aggravation.

'Look, Ryan, I'm tired,' she said, sounding ticked off rather than weary. 'Just tell me where the bathroom is and where to put my stuff and I'll hit the sack.'

'At four in the afternoon?'

'It's been a long day and, like I said, I'm tired.'

'So I'll make us some coffee.'

'I don't want any coffee—'

'Sure you do, K.C.; we both know you're addicted to the stuff.'

His patiently amused indulgence only stoked her anger. She wouldn't drink his damn coffee if he begged!

'I just want to use the bathroom, Ryan,' she said, realising the excuse for an escape had become a reality.

He shook his head ruefully. 'It's not good manners to come into someone's house and immediately ask to use the toilet.'

'It's not good manners to pee on their floor either!'

Propping himself between her and the door he'd

opened to kill the burglar alarm, he sent her a tormenting half-smile.

'*Ryan*, I'm not kidding here. I really need to go.'

'Where?'

'The bathroom, dammit!'

'Which one? You've got a choice of three—*four* if you count the *en suite* off the master bedroom.'

'The *nearest* one, you idiot!'

'How about I make you a deal, K.C.?' His ocean-blue eyes sparked with mischief. 'I'll tell you how to find the bathroom, if you promise to tell me what you think each room needs.'

'Chew razorblades,' she muttered, moving past him to the small door on the right. 'I'll find it myself,' she said, while giving him one last hard glance and opening the door. 'It's only a matter of opening a few doors and being able to recognise porcelain.'

'True, but the question is—*is time on your side?*'

I hope so! she thought, pivoting around and striding into—a huge walk-in storage cupboard! She swore, drawing hearty male laughter. Furious and embarrassed, she swung around and glared at Ryan's amusement.

'I'm sorry, miss,' he said, mimicking a game-show host. 'But that's *not* the lucky door! However, you do get a consolation prize just for being so darn cute!' Then he dipped his head and presented her with a quick but very effective kiss.

Stupefied beyond verbal or physical protest, Kirrily could merely allow herself to be guided through the double doors at the end of the hall. She barely had time to register anything about the room they entered, other than it, too, was devoid of furniture but had a fireplace, before Ryan's hands turned her head to the left.

'There,' he said, pointing to a door on her left, 'is a bathroom. And over there—' he motioned to the right '—is the kitchen. If you aren't at the breakfast bar in five minutes, I'll round up a search party.'

*   *   *

'The milk's off; can you handle your coffee black?' Ryan asked when Kirrily finally rejoined him in the kitchen.

It irked her that he could go from being a prize-winning pain in the rear one minute to the epitome of Mr Nice Guy the next. Even more frustrating was his knack of jerking her from one emotion to another with the minimum effort. Wishing it otherwise, she sighed heavily. 'Black's fine.'

'Sure? You make it sound like the ultimate sacrifice.'

'The way you make coffee, *drinking* it, regardless of colour, is the sacrifice.' His indignant look was too phoney to move her to apologise so she gave her attention to studying her surroundings.

As kitchens went, this one was pretty near luxurious. Every modern electrical gadget known to man which belonged in such a room was there, but utility hadn't been achieved at the expense of attractiveness, proof being the beautifully crafted rosewood cupboards with their leaded light inserts. Large, airy and well lit, the room still managed to offer a homey sort of comfort that appealed to Kirrily, even in the absence of curtains and the colourful knick-knacks which would have personalised it.

'Nice,' she said, with deliberate understatement, then, knowing she was being petty, smiled and added, '*Really* nice. So,' she said, strolling to the French windows at the end of the room, 'how come you've kept this house such a big secret?'

He frowned over the top of his mug. 'I haven't.'

'Then why didn't I know about it?'

'You're annoyed because I didn't tell you I was building a house?'

'Not annoyed, just…curious,' she said, though silently she owned up to being a tad disappointed. It seemed to indicate how far their friendship had drifted apart over

the last couple of years. 'It seems funny no one mentioned it to me.'

'Guess they thought you wouldn't be interested.'

'That's never stopped Mum before; usually she acts
like it's her God-given duty to keep me posted on every
breath you take,' she said drily. 'If nothing else, I'd have
expected her to be raving about how brilliantly clever
you are and how fabulous the house was.'

'No one's seen the house since the foundations were
laid, so that'd explain why she hasn't raved about *it*,' he
said. 'And I guess the reason she hasn't been extolling
my brilliance is she figured you already knew about it.'

'Oh, p-lease! Your ego is beyond belief, Ryan
Talbot!'

The knowledge that K.C.'s teasing and laughter
sounded better to him in this room than it ever had anywhere else hit Ryan like the proverbial ton of bricks.
Until now he'd believed the incomplete atmosphere of
the house was due solely to the lack of appropriate furnishings and, when he'd thought about it, he'd expected
the traditional flavour of the house to clash with K.C.'s
overt vivaciousness and devil-may-care attitude. He'd
been wrong on both counts. Her presence brought an
aura of completion that the addition of mere furnishings
never would. That she merged so well—in fact, seemed
essential to a home he'd designed purely to satisfy his
own soul—was disturbing.

His gaze followed her as she inspected the house's
construction and design with an inbred knowledge of the
building game. After opening several cupboards, she
backtracked to the refrigerator.

'Er, Ryan,' she said, 'I'm not sure I'll be comfortable
on this no-food diet you appear to favour.'

'I'll grab some basics when we go into town for dinner. Usually I just bring down what I need.'

'You come down here a lot?'

'When I can. I usually manage about every third weekend or so.'

'Were you planning to bring me down here while I was in Sydney, or is my presence here only the result of what's going on?'

Ryan knew that he wouldn't even have mentioned the house unless she'd brought it up, and he also knew that he wouldn't have brought her here even if she'd asked. He wasn't aware when or why he'd arrived at that subconscious decision, but he was beginning to suspect that on some level at least he must have known the impact she'd have on the house and, consequently, him.

'I never thought of bringing you here until we were on our way back from Sydney. Why?'

'Oh, no reason.'

He thought he saw a hint of hurt in her eyes, but she turned away before he could be sure.

'What's through here?'

'Laundry,' he said, wondering if the strain of keeping his distance showed in his voice.

'Can I look?' she asked.

'No.'

The flat refusal had her spinning to look at him. 'Why not? You said you'd show me around.'

'And you claimed you were too tired; a few minutes ago all you wanted to do was crawl into bed.'

'I guess the coffee helped.'

'Remarkably, since you haven't even tasted it.' Picking up the cup she'd left sitting on the table, he brought it to her.

Her gaze skittered guiltily from his. 'Er…thanks,' she managed, her fingers trembling from the innocuous contact with his. She raised the cup to her lips in the hope that caffeine would dull her reaction to his nearness. She took a mouthful of the liquid, but under Ryan's intense gaze almost choked trying to swallow it. His face contorted in instant concern and his hand closed around her wrist to prevent her making things worse with a too hurried second gulp.

'I...I'm OK,' she lied, her heart pounding as if trying to break out of her chest.

His brows pulled together and his blue eyes became assessing as they moved over her face. Unable to look away, she lifted her free hand and pushed her hair behind her shoulders, not from necessity but because she needed to convince herself that her paralysis was only mental. Yet when Ryan's fingers repeated the action the heat which coursed from her scalp to her toes must surely have done some really serious damage to her spinal cord.

'So,' he said, his jaw tight, as if he was struggling to keep his temper in check, 'I gather that you've now changed your mind and want a guided tour rather than to go to bed?'

Kirrily bit her tongue hard to stop the wanton response that rose in her mind and simply nodded. A muscle jerked at the side of his mouth, and as he moved to the other end of the kitchen with an angry rigidity she was fairly certain she'd heard him say, 'Pity!' She was about to tell him where he could take his moodiness when he pushed open a swing-door and, looking the picture of patience, indicated that she should follow.

'C'mon,' he said pleasantly. 'Bring your coffee with you.'

Kirrily told herself it was curiosity not the hundred-megawatt smile he produced which made her comply.

CHAPTER ELEVEN

CONSCIOUS of being watched as she mopped the last of the Bolognese sauce from her plate with the last of the garlic bread, and unable to ignore it any longer, Kirrily lifted her gaze to meet Ryan's amused one. His own plate empty, he lounged lazily in the corner of the booth they shared in the small but atmospheric restaurant he'd suggested for dinner.

'That's one of the things I like about you, K.C.,' he drawled. 'You're never shy around food.'

'Especially not Italian,' she said, resisting the urge to ask what he considered her other likeable traits to be. 'This place is good—equal to anywhere I've ever eaten on Lygon Street. Do you eat here a lot when you come down?'

'Not really. I only come down to work on the house, and usually I'm so bushed at the end of a day that getting dressed up to go out and eat on my own is too much hard work.' He grinned. 'Even for *great* Italian, although I'm sure you'd argue with me.'

Kirrily shook her head, dabbing her mouth with her napkin before speaking. 'Nope. I know exactly what you mean. Some days after being on the set from six in the morning until six at night I'm too exhausted to even fix myself a sandwich.' She sighed. 'But what I really hate after a hard day is having to dress up and be bright-eyed and bushy-tailed at some network function or fund-raiser that lasts until midnight. *Especially*—' she grimaced '—when I'm due in Make-up at five the next morning.'

'That happen often? The extra-curricular activities, I mean.'

'Too often. But then it goes with the territory, same as having your weekends consumed by shopping-centre promotions and the like.'

'Still, you must get paid pretty well for the extra hours.'

Kirrily's derisive laugh wasn't forced. 'Don't I wish! Unfortunately lowly little soap actors like me get a set wage, and all those extra commitments promoting the series are in my contract.'

Ryan watched silently as Kirrily bestowed one of her best smiles on the teenage waiter who brought their coffee. He noted the uncertain frown that gathered on the kid's brow as he, no doubt, tried to decide if K.C. really was who he thought she was. Ryan imagined the kitchen abuzz with, 'I'm sure that's the actress from that TV show... Nah! Couldn't be...' 'Let me serve 'em this time and I'll tell you...'

So far four different people had attended to them since they'd walked in forty-five minutes ago. It was getting to be more irritating than amusing.

'You realise you're the cause of a lot of speculation?' he asked, when the waiter couldn't legitimately delay at their table any longer and left.

She groaned. 'That, too, goes with the territory. Be grateful my character has been off the screen for a while or it might've been worse.'

'How so?'

'*Autographs,*' she whispered, looking about them furtively. 'Once in a restaurant a co-star and I had to sign about thirty. Our dates *weren't* impressed.'

'I don't blame them. They probably thought your private time was exclusively theirs.'

'Ha! My private time is rarely *mine.*'

'I have to admit I was ignorant of the extent of the demands on an actor's time,' he said.

An ironic smile nudged her mouth. 'It's kept secret to preserve the glamorous image of acting for the general public.'

'But the reality is it's more grit than glamour, huh?'

'A *lot* more.'

'Not to mention downright dangerous when you fall prey to a nutcase.'

Ryan's tone was coldly flat, but it was more than that which caused Kirrily to shiver. Her involuntary reaction pulled a muttered curse from the man opposite.

'K.C., have you thought about what you're going to do if they don't catch this guy?'

The fear that stiffened her face was a physical pain in Ryan's chest even after she'd camouflaged it behind bravado.

'They'll catch him,' she said.

'But what if they don't?' he persisted, playing the devil's advocate. 'Are you going to continue in a job that keeps you in the public eye? That potentially puts you at risk to not just this lunatic but *every* cretin who develops an obsession about your sexy little body and beautiful face.'

Her failure to respond made him want to shake her. 'Answer me, damn it!' he insisted. 'Are you?'

'I...I...I don't know. I mean, I like acting; I—'

'A moment ago you were complaining about long hours and lousy pay.'

'Well, yes...but...there are other factors.'

Ryan thought she sounded less than convinced. 'Such as?'

'It's *interesting*. Even after nearly two years it doesn't bore me the way all those other jobs I've had did. Before I got the role in *Hot Heaven* the longest I'd stayed in one job was two months.' Her chin lifted a notch. 'Acting's given me control of my life—'

'*Rubbish.*'

'Wh—?'

'That's rubbish and you know it!' he said, edging forward and leaning across the table. 'Moving to Melbourne was what gave you control of your life. Or at least what you perceived to be control. You took the role in *Hot Heaven* on impulse because it came at a time when you wanted to leave home but didn't want to hurt your folks by saying so. *Hot Heaven* gave you a legitimate reason for not just moving out but moving to a whole different state.' Even seeing the anger growing on her face wasn't enough to stop Ryan. 'Hell, I'll bet you never once considered becoming an actor until that male model who was panting after you conned you into going to that audition with him!'

'That's not true!' she denied, half rising to her feet.

'Isn't it?'

'No!'

There were mere inches between their noses, but Ryan couldn't have said how long they traded furious stares with each other, because at some point his anger got lost in the heady, exotic scent of her perfume and the emerald depths of her dark-lashed eyes.

The flickering glow of the candle highlighted her beautifully sculptured face, aiding and abetting the escape of memories he needed to imprison—memories of how she'd turned her soft cheek into his large, rough hand and rubbed against it, how her perfectly shaped lips had brushed, pressed and finally opened beneath his and how she'd all but purred with pleasure when his need to taste more of her had driven his mouth to explore lower. But mere memories couldn't distract him from the here and now, and his heart lurched in his chest at the radiant smile she offered him.

'For your information, Ryan, I went to that audition out of curiosity. I've never been *conned* into anything in my life.'

'Really?' The hint of smugness in her tone made him

add, 'So how do you explain ending up in Rich Nichols' car all those years ago?'

'My vulnerability to a blond-haired, blue-eyed guy I had a serious crush on.'

'Nichols has black hair.'

'I know,' she said softly. 'And I've no idea what colour *his* eyes are.'

'What about the male model?' he asked, knowing he shouldn't, despising the way his voice scratched.

She met his gaze for an endlessly long second. 'What male model?'

There was nothing scratchy about her voice; it curled around him like soft, spiralling smoke and set off alarms in his brain. Retreating into his seat as if burnt, although, given the temperature of his body, spontaneous self-combustion was probably more likely, Ryan signalled for the bill. He had to get out of there. *Now.*

Kirrily again tossed irritably onto her stomach and punched the pillow. Not that the pillow was the problem.

It was past two a.m. and here she was, wide awake on the sofa bed from hell, while Ryan 'wouldn't kiss her on a bet' Talbot was doubtlessly sleeping peacefully on the huge, king-size bed in the master bedroom. That there was a long, long hallway with four *unfurnished* bedrooms between them really irritated her! Surely it should have occurred to him to buy at least *one* decent bed to cater for guests? Of course, she was hardly a guest—more like a refugee to whom Ryan felt obligated to offer asylum; too bad his bed wasn't included in the deal!

Bad thought, Kirrily! Not, her brain told her, conducive to restful sleep.

'Yeah, right, kiddo,' she grumbled aloud. 'Like you really believe this dumb sofa is what's keeping you awake.'

With a heavy sigh, she swung her bare feet to the

ground, grateful for the underfloor heating system Ryan had incorporated into the house's design. Aided only by moonlight, she located her robe and, slipping it on, went to the window. She tried to use the rural silence and star-studded sky to calm her, but her mind was too pre-occupied.

She'd thought he was going to kiss her. No, she'd been *certain* he was going to kiss her. Heck, she'd practically *begged* him to kiss her! But instead he'd whisked them out of the restaurant as if all the devils and flames of hell were on his heels.

They'd arrived home twelve and a half silent minutes later, when he'd tossed a pillow and a set of clean sheets onto the sofa in the den and issued her a curt goodnight.

With hindsight Kirrily realised he'd been keeping his temper on a tight leash, and there were no prizes for guessing why. He'd obviously concluded that her be-haviour in the restaurant had been another cleverly thought out attempt at seduction. Well, he was *wrong*! It was clumsy, unintentional, and Kirrily hated herself for the way her body went into overdrive while her brain ceased all function around Ryan. Why did love have to be so damn humiliating? And *why*, curse it, did she have to fall for Ryan?

Groaning with frustration, she searched for a way of distracting her preoccupied mind. Usually when she couldn't sleep she sought refuge in hot chocolate and late-night movies to relax her, but as Ryan hated choc-olate and the only TV was a small portable in his room those options weren't available to her. Nor did she have a book to read or a script to learn. Desperate for activity, she headed to the door.

The hallway was eerily quiet, but showered in moon-light, courtesy of a floor-to-ceiling window outside the den and the skylight at the other end of the passage. Without bothering to switch on a light, Kirrily padded barefoot down its length, and at the sight of Ryan's closed bedroom door the breath she'd been holding escaped in a relieved rush. Mentally picturing him nude and spread-eagled across his mattress was one thing, but she was in no shape to deal with the reality of it. When her hand closed over the brass handle of the bathroom door, the slight click as it opened was so quiet that she felt it rather than heard it.

'Kirrily?'

Her heart leapt at the whisper of her name. *Ryan.*

'Are you all right?' he asked softly.

It took the length of several rapid, erratic heartbeats that had nothing to do with fear for her to nod, a few more to brace herself enough to turn and face him. He stood in his now open doorway, his features a haunting combination of shadows and highlights in the soft lunar glow, his bare chest, with its smattering of golden hair, a fascinating temptation of perfect planes and muscular mounds. Her heart seemed wedged in her throat, but its throbbing rhythm echoed in a lower region of her female anatomy.

'I…I'm…f-f-fine.' The words sounded unconvincing even to her, and though she couldn't see his eyes his statue-silent stance made her doubt he'd bought them either.

'Honest,' she reinforced. 'I just couldn't sleep. I think it's the quiet. I'm used to falling off to the sound of traffic and emergency sirens and…and things. I… thought a hot shower might help…sort of settle my restlessness…' Her babbling died out of her own brain's lack of interest, but when after long moments Ryan continued neither to move nor speak the smothering blanket of silence again propelled her to speech.

'I'm sorry if I woke you; I—'

'You didn't.' His voice was rough. 'I haven't been able to sleep either.'

'Oh…'

'Yeah,' he said drily. '*Oh.*'

There was a wealth of irony and frustration behind his words and Kirrily was alert to every bit of it.

'Do you *really* think a hot shower will work, K.C.?'

If it does, she thought, it'll be the biggest miracle performed with water since the parting of the Red Sea.

She shrugged. 'Well…it can't hurt any.'

'I suppose it's worth a thought,' he conceded. ''Cos cold ones don't help one damn bit. I should know; I've had three since we got home tonight.'

The obvious implication left her struggling for an intelligent response.

'Three long, cold showers,' he repeated, as if talking to himself. 'And I'm still on fire. I want you so bad I'm aching with it.'

His name left her lips, in a croaked whisper barely audible to her above the hammering of her heart and the mêlée of her hormones. Weak-kneed, she sagged against the wall, hoping it would keep her upright as the blood swirled through her body at the speed of light and her lungs could only manage shallow sucks of air. Yet despite the sensation of not being able to breathe she didn't pretend that her gasp at Ryan's four-letter expletive was a reaction to anything but the sexual connotation it evoked.

'There's got to be at least a hundred reasons why I shouldn't take you in my arms right this minute.' Though he hadn't moved, his groaned words and the semi-darkness seemed to reduce the four feet of space between them to mere millimetres, charging the atmosphere with a claustrophobic sensuality. 'Tell me the reasons, K.C.,' he urged. 'Remind me why I should step back into my room and lock the door when what I want to do is grab you and make love to you until neither of us can stand up.'

Clenching her fists, Kirrily tried to fight against the tempest of emotion swamping her. Damn you, she wanted to scream. I ache too! Too much to be your conscience! But anger and frustration were like hands around her throat, wringing hot, silent tears from her eyes, making words impossible; braced against the wall, all she managed were two slow shakes of her head.

In a heartbeat he was in front of her, lifting her chin with fingers that trembled, until her eyes connected with his.

'Ah, honey, *don't*,' he pleaded, cupping her head in his hands with infinite gentleness. 'Please don't cry... Dear God, I'd rather your anger than your tears.'

The tenderness with which his lips touched her lashes was in stark contrast to the desperation in his words.

'Don't cry, angel... I'm sorry... I'd die before... before I'd make...you cry.'

To Kirrily the disjointed but caring endearments muttered between gentle kisses felt like salvation. And as his mouth continued to travel her face, absorbing her salty tears, anger and frustration gave way to a hope that started in her heart and was pumped to every fibre of her body; instinct demanded she follow her heart...

Surprise arrested Ryan's movements when a deliciously sweet mouth brushed his own, but just one slow stroke of that same tongue across his lower lip was enough to reactivate him. With a sigh of gratitude his hand caught the back of her neck and, angling her head to his best advantage, he sought the deeper pleasures of her mouth.

While his ravenous need for this woman was still inimitable, the discovery of a sweeter but equally rapacious hunger within Kirrily herself left him quaking. The sensations that stirred within him as her body sagged into his almost undid him.

'Oh, Ryan...' Her breathing was as ragged as his, her green eyes slumberous with desire. 'I...I...'

As he smiled at her bemused expression, his hands skimmed her shoulders and the curve of her neck without any conscious directive from him.

'You are so beautiful,' he whispered. 'So perfectly, perfectly beautiful and innocent.'

She raised an amused eyebrow. 'Innocent? You're obviously forgetting last night.'

'I only wish I could.'

Neither his tone nor expression were light-hearted, and disappointment chilled Kirrily. 'You regret last night?' But even as she voiced the question she could see he did. Humiliated, she tried to pull away from him. The wall and his hold on her shoulders defeated her effort.

'I don't mean—'

'Let me go!'

'Kirrily, I—'

She fought to distance herself from him, but Ryan's superior strength triumphed and within seconds she was trapped against his chest, her arms secured against her sides.

'Listen to me,' he said. 'What I regret about last night are the circumstances and the way I treated you.'

With his laboured sigh reverberating through her, Kirrily found herself almost afraid to anticipate his next words. The touch of his hand on her cheek was feather-soft as it crept to her jaw and exerted gentle pressure until she was looking into his eyes.

'Last night I was on hormone overload and not tuned in to *my* emotions, much less yours. I hurt you, I—'

'You didn't. I mean…well, I expected it to hurt a bit.'

'Oh, sweetheart, I don't just mean the act itself, I mean my anger, my accusations…' He shook his head in a gesture of ironic despair. 'It was so much less than you deserved, honey, and there aren't words to tell you how sorry I am for that.' He drew a languorous finger across her bottom lip. 'But I swear I'll make you forget it.'

Didn't he realise his concern was misplaced? That even if she hadn't felt as she did about him she'd remember every detail of what they'd shared? 'Ryan, a woman's first experience of lovemaking isn't something that's easily forgotten.'

'Well, I'm making damn sure yours will *never* be,' he returned, lowering his head, and he brushed his lips lightly across hers.

She wasn't sure what caused her brain the most confusion—his kisses or his words. 'But…but you just said you *were* going to make me forget it.'

'Uh-uh,' he muttered, showering her face with butterfly kisses. 'I said I'd make you forget what happened *last night*.'

Hands on his chest, she levered herself out of reach of his teasing lips and frowned up at him. 'Yeah,' she said. 'And last night you made love to me for the first time.'

He shook his head, startling her even more by swinging her into his arms. 'Uh-uh, honey. Last night we had *sex*—'

The sudden break in his voice drew her eyes back to his; the intensity in them scorched her soul.

'Tonight I'll make *love* to you,' he said huskily. 'And it'll be the first time…for *both* of us.'

CHAPTER TWELVE

KIRRILY was so totally focused on the sensation of being in Ryan's arms that her grip on him automatically tightened and she uttered a disappointed 'oh' as her legs were lowered and her feet connected with the earthy roughness of a hand-woven rug.

'Two seconds, sweetheart, OK?' he whispered.

'OK,' she agreed, disappointment vanishing with his light kiss and a smile full of sensual promises. Moments later the room's dimness was overpowered as the light in the adjoining *en suite* bathroom was turned on.

Earlier today, when Ryan had taken her through the house, Kirrily had forced herself to view it dispassionately. Now, warmed by desire and need and on the threshold of making love to Ryan, she wanted to stamp every detail of it into her mind: the two sets of French windows through which the morning sun would awaken their love-drenched bodies, the large crafted mirror atop the oak tallboy, which even in the muted light reflected the excitement and passion of her eyes, the high-backed chair where the clothes Ryan had worn to dinner lay in disarray.

She smiled. Ryan was usually pedantically neat, and that he'd been too strung out over *her* to hang his clothes up after they'd returned from dinner appealed to her feminine pride. An even more feminine part of her sent her eyes in the direction of the king-size, four-poster carved oak bed. The duvet was on the floor, the top sheet twisted like rope and the top corner of the fitted sheet unhooked to display the mattress warranty. Its appearance was more post lovemaking than pre. Did helping your lover make his bed *before* you actually got to sleep in it come under the heading of foreplay? Chuckling softly, she began straightening it.

'What's so funny?'

She turned her head, intending to reply, but the action of Ryan flipping two condoms onto the bedside table temporarily froze her tongue. There was a possessive gleam in his eyes most feminists would have deplored, but to Kirrily's astonishment it thrilled her all the way to her toes.

'Your bed looks like the aftermath of an orgy,' she said finally, hoping she appeared more at ease than she was. How come last night she'd been able to vamp it up and now she was as nervous as a virgin at a bikers' convention? She turned back to the task of righting the bed, but her movements were clumsy as anticipation hummed through her, and the sheets were instantly forgotten when male arms entrapped her from behind and she was drawn back against Ryan's solid male frame.

'You don't have any idea what the aftermath of an orgy looks like,' he teased.

Her breath caught as his fingers began to uncinch the tie of her robe. 'T-t-true,' she managed. 'But I've got a good imagination.'

'Me too,' Ryan muttered, his breath warm against the curve of her neck as he nuzzled the robe from her shoulders. 'Which is why the bed's a shambles.'

The feel of towelling slipping down her arms was so sensual that the material might easily have been the finest silk.

'Lord, you're beautiful! So damn beautiful...'

He kissed her shoulder with such soft reverence that Kirrily's breath caught, but the touch of his hands at her hips, guiding her body from his so that the bulky garment could continue its drop to the floor, left her trembling. She sagged back against him, glorying in his guttural groan and the tightening of his arms across her abdomen. But she wanted to be closer. *Needed* to be closer. Much closer.

For too long Ryan had worn a 'Look, Don't Touch' sign, now that it was gone she wanted to indulge her sense of touch to the point of overdose! What she craved was to wrap her arms around him, around his naked, muscled torso so they were skin to skin and the wiry coarseness of his chest hair was grating against her breasts; she wanted to walk her fingers over every millimetre of his smooth mahogany skin and watch his nipples grow as erect as hers. She wanted to run her tongue across his perfect white teeth until he bit it to stillness and she wanted to watch his face contort in pleasure as his body, heart and soul joined with hers.

Shivering with the potency of her own thoughts, she tried to turn, but her effort was thwarted by superior male strength.

'Uh-uh,' he said huskily. 'Be still.'

'Uh-uh?' she echoed in disbelief, shivering as he buried his face in her hair at the nape of her neck.

'I'm not letting you turn around.'

'Ry…an.'

He chuckled at her obvious protest. 'We're taking this slow and easy; they're the rules. I'm going to do this right even if it kills me.'

Ryan and his stupid rules! she thought, every nerve-ending in her body rioting as he scattered kisses over her shoulders. *She* was the one that this slow torture was going to kill! She was tempted to elbow him in the guts and turn anyway, but suddenly the notion of actually *stopping* the sensual adoration of his mouth across her shoulders struck her as pure insanity!

'Lean forward…' he directed, murmuring his approval as her head lowered obediently and she pulled her hair out of the way.

His hot, busy mouth continued its seductive assault until Kirrily was convinced he wanted to melt her bones one by one. Certain she'd collapse at any moment, and seeking support, she reached back, grabbing his thighs, and encountered firm masculine legs encased in denim. Yet her groan wasn't entirely based in disappointment as he moved and brushed his arousal across her bare buttocks.

'Ry...an,' she gasped as he unlocked one arm from around her to employ a hand to caress her side from thigh to armpit. 'Sh-shouldn't you at least...uh...?' Words and thought evaporated as the wandering hand drifted over her abdomen, seemingly uncertain as to whether it would move up or down. Mentally she tried to will it in both directions at once as the demands of her throbbing breasts merged with the slick hunger between her thighs.

'Shouldn't I what?' Ryan asked, marvelling that he could even form the question, much less get it out. Even doing nothing more than simply holding her and touching her in the most innocent of places he was burning up from the inside out!

'Ah...shouldn't you...take your jeans off?'

A moan of anguish burst from him when her question was accompanied by the wriggling of her small, firm butt against his groin. Determined to stay in control and halt the titillating action, Ryan instinctively repositioned his hands. It proved a poorly considered defence...

Kirrily bucked as his hands clamped flat against her body, his thumbs pressed low on her abdomen, his fingers immersed in the triangle thatch of hair at the apex of her thighs. She heard him suck in what she suspected was a steadying breath and envied him; she couldn't even remember *how* to breathe. And as he continued to ply his magic the temperature of her body soared to the point where her blood must surely have been white-hot.

'Please, Ryan…' Her words were tinged with pathos and need.

'Please… what?' His voice was as strained and uneven as her own and she felt a shudder go through him, but her response was distracted by the movement of his hands on her stomach. Back and forward… Up and down… He continued with the sweet torment until Kirrily was certain a squadron of butterflies was rioting inside her. Back and forth… Up and down…

Down, dammit, down! her mind silently screeched, even as some region of her brain urged her to be patient, told her that bit by microscopic bit Ryan's fingers *were* creeping closer to where she most wanted them. Yet her rapidly spiralling passion was all too eager to ignore patience and any other so-called virtues!

'Touch me,' she begged, knowing he felt the fluttery contractions he was creating within her belly. Her head flopped back against his shoulder and she lifted her eyes to his face. '*Hold* me. Oh, Ryan, please? *Please*, hol—' The rest of her plea was captured by Ryan's mouth.

Her lips had barely touched his before Ryan felt his heart unravel with the force and power of what he felt for this woman. Surpassing the mere physical and transcending the emotional, the emotion flowed within him as fiercely and strongly as his own blood. And, like his blood, it was heated by the ardent exploration Kirrily was making in his mouth. He'd long suspected that K.C. could fray the edges of his emotions and provoke him to passion, but the discovery that he had an identical effect on her still threw him.

For long, deliciously sweet moments his male ego was content to allow her the aggressive lead, to be seduced by her tongue and delighted by the frustrated sounds escaping from her as she writhed to find what she most sought. The more she gave, the more desperately aroused she became, and the more Ryan encouraged her. Then suddenly, in Ryan's mind, the needle on his mental sensuality gauge, which was supposed to indicate who was in control, began spinning wildly in all directions!

Discovering he was trembling from head to foot, Ryan frantically shifted his weight to balance Kirrily more firmly against his left thigh. Then, praying his own body would withstand the pleasure he sought to give hers, he plunged his tongue into the sweet, moist cavern of her mouth at the same momentous instant that his fingers discovered an equally warm, moist part of her.

Kirrily was grateful for the strong male arm that stopped her from collapsing, but gratitude drowned in the waves of coloured heat radiating from the rhythm of Ryan's hand, touching her as she'd willed it to do, warming her as only he could. Instinctively she tried to move closer to it, needing more of his touch, more of the magic of its rhythm.

Ah, the rhythm! The rhythm was everywhere—in her heart, in her body, and in the warm masculine chest that pillowed her thrashing head. A pagan, primal rhythm, which grew louder and louder until she was almost afraid it would deafen her. No, not deafen, *devour* her—consume her body entirely, leaving her limp and lifeless but blissfully fulfilled. Yes, fulfilment—that was what Ryan was offering her, what he was urging her to seek with his whispered words of, 'Go with it, sweetheart... Let it happen... I want to feel you melt...'

Inspired by the husky encouragement and no longer able to deny herself the pleasure within her grasp, Kirrily shut herself down to everything but the rhythm...

The gasped cry of his name as her body quaked in climax threatened to push Ryan's precariously balanced control over the edge. Gritting his teeth, he held her with one arm until her body ultimately stilled, while the other worked feverishly to unbutton his jeans. Though he'd initially cursed the fact he wasn't wearing a zippered pair, the concentration the action required fortunately drew him at least a fraction further from what any man could only have described as a premature disaster. Bending slightly, he shoved them to his knees, using his feet to work them off the rest of the way.

'Thank you.'

Her breathless words brought his head up; her angelic smile threatened to pull him back to the edge. Yet the need to taste her again had him pushing his luck and allowing her to turn in his arms.

'My pleasure,' he whispered against her mouth, 'is your pleasure.'

If kisses were cars this one could have claimed zero to three hundred kilometres an hour in *nothing flat*! he decided as they tumbled as one onto the bed. Despite his intentions to keep things simmering sensually slowly for as long as possible, one touch of her tongue against his propelled the situation to erotic boiling point. Their mouths fused, their lungs surviving on only abrupt snatches of desire-laden air, they rolled first one way then the other, adding further to the bed's state of disarray.

Having her nudity pressed top to toe against his own was like being wrapped in hot silk. Living, breathing silk, which fluttered beneath his fingers. She purred deep in her throat when his lips and tongue laved her neck. It was a magnificent neck; arched, it was the perfect foil to highlight her perfectly formed breasts with their succulent rosebud tips.

The tug of Ryan's mouth against her breast jerked Kirrily's body around as if he were a million volts of electricity; without any conscious command her legs pulled up until he stretched between the valley of her thighs, just as his face was pressed between the valley of her breasts. To her heart the warmth and weight of his body upon her was a gift from the gods, a treasure she'd been too afraid to search for in the past. Yet Ryan was intermingling his soul-destroying kisses with mutterings of praise that made *her* feel treasured.

She moaned as again his mouth worshipped her breasts while his hands skimmed her body with feather-light strokes that were as exciting as they were frustrating. He was being so gentle, *too* gentle, and she wanted to scream, not for release but at him! Yet in that very instant her feelings for this man were suddenly so *strong*, so *clear* that she wondered how she'd ever been able to conceal them. She loved him with every fibre of her being, with every atom of emotion she'd ever known, would *ever* know. Nothing would ever connect with her soul as Ryan did; what she felt for him was as infinite and intangible as time itself.

'Sweet, sweet Kirrily...' he praised her, his mouth moving to her ribs. 'Tell me what you want.' He lifted his head, his face lined with the same urgency she'd heard in his voice. 'I want to love you as you've never been loved before. I want this time to be special.'

Though she appreciated he was bound and determined to do whatever was physically necessary to make this time better than the first, he needed to understand that for her *every* time would be beyond compare. Smiling, she tugged at his hair, encouraging him into kissing range.

'I just want *you*,' she told him, her hands holding his face. 'No holds barred.' She kissed the confused frown marring his brow. 'I'm not made of china, Ryan; I won't break.'

She followed up her words with a kiss that couldn't possibly be misunderstood and destroyed what little was left of Ryan's mind and self-control. Never once lifting his lips from the soft, pliant ones of the woman whose hands were scalding his skin, he groped blindly about the top of the bedside table till his fingers encountered a square of cool foil. Only then did he lever himself upright.

'Let me!'

The breathy command came at the same time as swift

feminine fingers snatched the sealed condom from his own, trembling ones. He better than anyone knew that K.C. didn't appreciate his taking it solely upon himself to protect her.

Rolling onto his side, he propped himself on one elbow and studied Kirrily's unselfconscious nude perfection as she sat up. His idle hand began tracing a path along the inside of her thigh and she jerked in response.

'Stop it!' She frowned. 'You're distracting me.'

He shrugged. 'Distractions are allowed; it's "no holds barred", remember? Just out of curiosity, do you know what you're doing?' he asked.

Flicking her hair over her shoulder, she gave him her best smirk. 'Oh, yeah,' she whispered. 'I know exactly what I'm doing.' Then with her gaze locked on his she seductively ran her tongue along the edge of the packet, then ripped it open with her teeth.

Ryan swore and lunged across her, trapping her wrist in a firm grip.

'Um, I'm not sure,' she said hesitantly, 'but I think you'll have to get up again so I can put it on.'

'The hell you will!'

Taking the condom from her now suspiciously pliant hand, Ryan eased back and commenced sheathing himself, the knowledge that she watched his every movement as arousing as it was unnerving. When he raised his head from the completed task, it was easy to see that Kirrily too had found watching him pleasurable.

'I *thought* that was how they worked,' she said, pure devilment dancing in her emerald eyes. 'But I guess you thought I'd do it wrong, huh?'

'Yeah,' he growled, pushing her onto her back. 'So wrong you'd be named one of the ten most potent causes of premature ejaculation!'

The laughter his comment provoked died the moment his hand parted her thighs. For Ryan the glazed pleasure in her eyes as he checked her readiness was as erotic as her body's slick eagerness. Awash with emotions stronger than any he'd ever experienced, he stroked her in time with his rapidly beating heart.

Even in the indirect light from the *en suite* bathroom, her beauty was radiant enough to steal his breath. He looked at the long, silky darkness of her hair against the mattress and wanted to cocoon himself in it. He looked at her slightly parted mouth and tasted its sweetness in his own. On a groan he lowered himself over her body, intending only to possess again that sweet, tempting mouth, but he saw his soul in her desire-clouded eyes and in that instant he was both lost…and found.

Kirrily's heart and hips lurched as one in a connection that was as spiritual as it was physical, and it was a toss-up whether the rightness of what she was feeling would show itself as laughter or tears.

'Don't close your eyes,' Ryan urged, his face mirroring her own awe.

'I won't,' she promised, her vision blurring as she met his intense blue gaze. 'Oh…Ryan, it's…' She snatched an unsteady breath. 'It's so…' Clutching his shoulders, she rose to meeting his slow-building thrusts.

'So…what?' he asked, his tongue catching an errant tear.

With desire, passion and love swamping her from all directions, Kirrily struggled to find the right words. She shook her head, more bemused than frustrated. 'It's…it's…'

'What?' he repeated, his fingers interlocking with hers, his face showing the pleasurable strain that she too was feeling.

'It's…' She was fighting to keep her eyes open against the intense sensations bombarding her body and brain. 'Oh!' she gasped as her body bucked. 'Oh… Ryan…Ry—'

'Damn,' he groaned, his body tensing, yet his gaze

still locked on hers. 'You feel so-o-o good! So...so right...'

Hot, emotional heat spiralled within her. 'You belong,' she gasped, her internal muscles gripping him as fiercely as her fingers did his shoulders. 'Oh...yes! Yes! Ryan...'

'Look at me!' His breathy command forced her lashes up. 'Watch...' he said as their hips crashed against each other's. 'See...see what you...do to me...'

They erupted together in an explosion so spectacular that Ryan continued to shake long after his release. For an endless time he was incapable of doing anything more than let his sweat-slick body remain over Kirrily's. When it dawned on him that he was probably crushing her, he immediately eased himself onto his back and drew her against him, too spent to do anything more than hold her warmth to him.

Snuggling closer to the damp, naked male body, Kirrily closed her eyes and tried to survive on what little oxygen her lungs could draw from the passion-drenched air. She'd heard it said that the French called orgasm 'little death'; she well understood why. A shiver hit her as the winter chill gained ascendency over her slowly cooling internal heat.

'Cold?' Ryan asked.

'Actually I think it's shock,' she said, nuzzling closer to his solid male warmth as he settled the duvet over them. 'I never imagined anything could be so...so powerful, so...I don't know... *cosmic*.' She angled her head more comfortably in the curve of his arm so she could see his face. 'I guess this is why the term "better than sex" was originated, huh?'

His expression seemed to absorb her. 'Yeah,' he said, touching a lazy finger against her lower lip. 'I'd say that's possibly how the term was born.'

'Only *possibly*?'

'Mmm, unlike you, K.C., I've never been one to jump

to hasty conclusions *and*—' pressure from his finger across her mouth stopped her from voicing an objection to the accusation '—based on such limited research, I'm reluctant to firmly commit myself to an answer one way or the other.'

'Ah,' she said, forcing down a grin. 'So how much research do you think it would require for you to…you know, commit yourself?'

'Hard to say; scientists have been known to research a subject for years and years.'

Ryan's tone might have been casual, but the look in his eyes was as carnal as the way his finger moved down her neck to rest at the base of her throat.

'Beautiful,' he muttered, replacing the finger with his lips. 'Bone-achingly beautiful.'

He'd only kissed her throat, yet somehow every nerve-ending in her body was tingling.

'Tell me, Kirrily,' he said huskily, his hands playing over her shoulders. 'You ever been interested in being a research assistant?'

She shook her head, struggling with the excitement he was activating within her as he drew a slow finger between the valley of her breasts.

'Science was never my strong suit. Is it interesting?'

'Oh, yeah,' he said, watching her eyes. 'Better than sex.'

She laughed. 'In that case, Professor, I'm all yours…'

CHAPTER THIRTEEN

WITH Ryan's breath soft at her neck, his chest warm against her back and his lower body spooned firmly around her own, Kirrily welcomed the intrusion of the morning's sun with a blissful sigh. The male hand pressed to her abdomen slid from there to tease the underside of her breast.

'Mmm,' she purred, nuzzling closer.

'Mmm, what?'

'Mmm, more,' she responded, her body wakening more quickly than her brain.

'More what?' The question was as teasing as his touch.

She sighed, rolling onto her back. Opening her eyes, she stroked a fascinated finger along his bristled jaw. 'More *everything*,' she said, loving the way desire darkened his eyes as he looked at her, but disappointed by his slowly shaking head.

'It's too soon,' he told her gently. 'You'll be sore and I don't want to hurt you.'

'You'd never hurt me, Ryan.' Her confidence was absolute, his answering smile pleased.

'But you're still sore,' he insisted, his fingers weaving themselves through her hair.

'Not *that* sore.' She grinned. 'Besides...' Her knuckles skimmed the inside of his thigh. 'I think you could produce the salve needed to cure me.'

One blonde eyebrow shot up. 'You're wanton, Kirrily Cosgrove.'

'Wantin' *you*, Ryan Talbot!' she retorted.

With lightning-fast aggression, Ryan was pulled into a kiss he had no inclination to resist even had he been capable of it.

Kirrily—spirited, impulsive and utterly irresistible. He thought she tasted even sweeter in the early sunlight than she had only hours before, but it had to be the hangover of passion; for surely nothing could be more deliciously intoxicating than the eager, responsive sensuality which had flowed from her as he'd loved her.

Loved her.

Yes, he loved her. Admitting as much had been a battle, but he only had to be hit over the head by his heart a few million times for him to realise that denial of the truth was futile.

Reality: Ryan Talbot had fallen in love with Kirrily Cosgrove and nothing on earth, past or present, would alter that.

He deepened the kiss, as a defence against his over-powering need to say the words—to tell her. Just as he'd done a dozen times during their night of lovemaking. He didn't want to frighten her or make her feel pressured. Didn't want her inexperience and impulsiveness auto-matically to voice reciprocal feelings.

Ah, hell! Who was he trying to kid? He wasn't being noble or considerate, he was being a *coward*! The thought that she *wouldn't* respond with 'I love you too' chilled him to the core.

His sudden withdrawal startled Kirrily. 'Ryan?' she said hesitantly as he sat up. 'What's up?'

The sun streaming through the French windows made his tousled hair sparkle six shades of gold and his broad bare back glisten. Her action in touching that back, when he silently shook his head, was only marginally conso-latory.

'Ryan…tell me. What's the matter?'

He weighed up the choice between fobbing her off

and baring his soul only for as long as it took for her to place a soft, tender kiss on his shoulder.

'This is probably going to scare you to death, but...' He sucked in a do-or-die breath. 'I'm in love with you.'

'I know.'

Her matter-of-fact tone spun him around. 'You *know*?'

She was fighting a smile and nodding. 'Trevor Nichols told me.'

'Trev... How...? What...?'

'But I'm not scared,' she continued over his incoherent stammering. 'You might make me tremble, but not with fear.' Rising to her knees, her nudity looking like sculptured perfection, she took his face between her hands and brushed her lips over his with angelic lightness. 'I love you too,' she whispered. 'I fell in love with you so long ago, Ryan, I can't even remember it happening.'

'You're in love with me?' He hardly dared believe it.

'Since before I was born.'

Groaning with relief, he collapsed them both back onto the mattress. As it had the night before, their lovemaking ran the gamut of emotions from passion to playfulness, their breathless sighs intermingled with lighthearted laughter, talking and teasing...

'You knew I loved you because *Trevor Nichols* said so!'

'Get over it, Ryan. He did us a favour.'

'How's that?'

Kirrily raised her head from her oral exploration of his belly and frowned at him. 'Do you honestly think I'd have thrown myself at you that night in the hotel if I hadn't known you loved me?'

'Aha! So you'll admit *you* came on to *me* that night?'

Her smirk was pure challenge. 'Make me...'

For the next four days the unexpectedness and newness of having Ryan love her and be her lover kept Kirrily content; there was something deliciously exciting about being cloistered away in a huge rural house with nobody knowing their whereabouts.

Yet, much as she might have wished otherwise, they weren't without the distractions of the outside world. Ryan had arranged for all calls to his home number to be automatically diverted to the Bowral house so both the police and the staff at Talbot's could contact him readily. Although it seemed to her that it was *Ryan* who was initiating all the contact with both, with his calling first the police and then the office within fifteen minutes of getting up and both at least twice more during the day.

More and more she felt an edginess in him that she sensed had to do with more than the police's clichéd responses such as, 'The matter is still under investigation; there have been no further developments,' or 'We'll advise you of any progress,' and his concern about how the office was coping in his absence. On several occasions she'd caught him in silent, deep introspection, and though his distraction had vanished the moment he'd seen her Kirrily couldn't help thinking his ready smiles were a tad too ready, too perfect, that he was trying to shield her from whatever was bothering him. She tried to tell herself she was imagining it, that, as he had finally recognised and accepted her as not just a woman but his lover, Ryan's need to protect her was no longer an issue. But his reluctance to confide in her was again brought home on Friday.

They'd spent a carefree morning scouring the antiques shops in nearby Mittagong, and arrived home with a partially restored steamer chest, which Kirrily had convinced Ryan would make a brilliant coffee-table for the living room. Though initially doubtful, Ryan had finally agreed to the purchase, expressing surprise at Kirrily's haggling skills.

'I'm a skilled negotiator,' she told him when they

walked into the kitchen, dumping the fresh bread rolls and honeyed ham they'd brought home for lunch on the counter.

'More like a con artist,' he returned, tweaking her nose affectionately.

She slapped his hand away. 'Half the fun of shopping for used furniture is the haggling.'

His hands went to her hips, drawing her nearer. 'So what's the other half?'

She grinned. 'After today, I'd say watching you try not to look guilty after I get them to agree my price.'

He laughed. 'You're incorrigible.'

'And you're *insatiable*.' But her complaint was half-hearted and she was already leaning towards his kiss. Her sigh at the sudden intrusion of the phone was heavy with disappointment.

'Hold that thought,' Ryan muttered, releasing her after a too brief peck.

She did, but within moments she'd sussed out that the call was going to be a lengthy one and set about preparing lunch. Lost in her own thoughts about the cosmic perfection she'd discovered in Ryan's arms, she was pulled back into reality by a loud string of explicit comments about architects with more creativity than common sense. Oblivious to her attention, Ryan slammed down the receiver, then raked both hands through his hair. Despite the accompanying colourful verbal tirade, the action spoke more of frustration than anger.

'Problem at the office?' she asked.

'Huh? No. No, it's nothing any halfway decent builder couldn't deal with. Ron has it under control.' The edge in his words was too sharp to be ignored.

'But you feel it's your responsibility and you should go to Sydney anyway.'

His gaze focused hard on her. 'Talbot's *is* my responsibility, K.C. The buck stops with me.'

At the lecturing tone of his voice she set the knife

aside. 'Why is it that whenever you slip into your Mr Responsibility mode I go back to being K.C.?'

'Pardon?'

'The first time we became lovers you called me *Kirrily*,' she said. 'I don't even think you were aware of it. And now you call me that nearly all the time except when—'

'When I call you honey or sweetheart or gorgeous... But I never call you *babe*.' He grinned, moving around the breakfast bar and stalking towards her. 'You hate guys calling you babe.'

His hands on her waist, he pulled her hips against his and nuzzled her neck. 'You smell good.'

She sighed. 'And you're trying to distract me.'

'Nah, I'm trying to get into your pants.'

Despite herself, she giggled. '*Ryan*, I'm trying to make lunch and have a conversation with you.'

'Darn. And here I am trying to make time and have sex with you.' He sighed heavily, his face serious. 'OK, I give in... You were saying?' His grin was sinful.

'Forget it,' she muttered. After all, she had...it was so damned hard to think with his hand slipping into her scanty knickers...

In the darkness of the early hours Ryan replaced the receiver on the bedside phone, grateful he'd been awake to answer it before it had woken Kirrily. Easing himself back onto the mattress, he stared at the ceiling. He'd grown up believing that falling in love made everything in a man's life perfect, yet his own had become a bloody mess that was only going to get worse.

He'd always envisaged that he'd be totally honest about every aspect of his past if ever he fell in love, that he'd have no secrets from the woman he chose to share his future with and that with her love and understanding he would, in time, be able to forgive himself, if not forget. Such idealistic expectations might have been feasible if he'd fallen for anyone other than Kirrily Claire Cosgrove, but, because he hadn't, the truth, be it told or concealed, could only be destructive to their love simply because of who Kirrily was and what he'd done.

Their love had no future.

'Why?' he whispered hoarsely, emotion again tearing him apart. 'Why *her*?' Turning his head, he glanced at her peaceful, sleeping face, helpless to prevent his knuckles brushing the softness of her cheek. 'Why me? Hell, Kirrily, why pick me?'

After they'd made love tonight, she'd asked him where they went from here, and hadn't been distracted by his teasing reply of, 'Sleep'. So he'd mumbled something about it being better not to make emotional decisions while she was under threat from a maniac and reluctantly she'd admitted he was right. Then, after blessing him with another dose of her sweet, trusting passion and declarations of love, she'd drifted into a peaceful sleep while he lay awake battling with his own cowardice and the demons of his past.

Though he could almost excuse what they'd shared in the hotel in Melbourne as being lust-driven, allowing what had happened since had been a conscious decision. Not the decision of a *clear* conscience, but a pure-hearted one based on hope's phantom whispers that love conquered all. That was the trouble with hope: it had a way of deafening you to the more experienced voice of reality. And the reality was that while he'd never *told* a lie to Kirrily their entire relationship was based on her ignorance of the truth.

He'd been living on borrowed time—no! *Stolen* time—because only he'd known that when it was safe for Kirrily to leave here what they'd shared would end. And it was safe *now*; the police had caught the man responsible.

Awaking alone and without the gentle loving that had greeted her every morning since they'd come to Bowral left Kirrily strangely unsettled. The concern etched on Ryan's face when she found him in the kitchen didn't lessen the sensation.

'Ryan…?' she said, puzzled to find him already showered and dressed when their only plans for the day had been to hang around the house. 'What's up? Why—?'

'They've caught him, Kirrily.'

'What?'

'The police have caught the guy who's been stalking you. Except you weren't the target…your flatmate Cathy was. The guy's name is Conrads. Wes Conrads—'

'Wait up!' The speed and the detached voice in which Ryan had fired the information at her made it hard to assimilate. '*Cathy* was the victim all along, not me? I…I don't understand.'

He sighed as if she were the bane of his life. 'Apparently Conrads was obsessed with her. It was the announcement of her engagement that caused him to freak out and blow up the car which he thought was hers because—'

'Because I let her drive it sometimes. And I can understand the house, since he must have known she lived there, but why the letters about me to the studio? Cath is an actor, sure, but we didn't work for the same network.'

'Apparently Conrads saw you as a corrupting influence on Cathy. And that's as much as I know. Believe me, at twenty past two in the morning just hearing the guy was nabbed was enough for me. If you want more information you can call Senior Sergeant Maskowski in Melbourne.' He inclined his head towards the phone. 'You can call him from here, but get dressed first so I can pack the car while you're doing it.'

'Pack the—?' It struck her then that each time she'd taken a step nearer him he'd taken two away. At this point the breakfast bar separating them seemed less of an obstacle than Ryan's detached formality. 'Ryan, what the hell's going on?'

'We're going back to Sydney.'

'*Now?* Just like...' she snapped her fingers '...*that*?'

'Kirrily, they've *got* the guy.' He said it as if she were a simpleton. 'There's no reason for you to even stay in Sydney, much less here. If you want to spend a few extra days, feel free, but if you don't hurry up and get dressed so I can pack the—'

'What's the all-fire hurry to pack the car?' she demanded. 'We've got *two overnight* bags between us; it's not like it's going to be an all-day task!'

He offered no response, already walking away from her, the action holding a symbolism she didn't want to acknowledge. Fear gripped her heart.

'Ryan!' Her voice held a touch of panic that she tried to quell as he stared back at her. 'Where are you going? What are you going to do?'

His expression was closed to her in a way she wouldn't have thought possible. In fact had it not been for the way his jaw suddenly clenched then unclenched she'd have said she was staring at a statue.

'Kirrily, if you're coming I'm leaving in thirty minutes.'

Her gut knotted. 'And if I'm not?'

'Then I'm leaving now. It's over, Kirrily.'

In her distraught state, Kirrily couldn't say how long she wandered the empty house crying, but she was standing in one of the unfurnished bedrooms when she made the decision to stop. Well, at least, *try* and stop, she amended as she fought a potential wail into a subdued sob/sniffle.

'So *this* is heartbreak,' she murmured aloud, experiencing what more seasoned actors often described as 'the third eye'—the ability to stand away from oneself and examine what one was feeling...

On a superficial physical level her head ached and her

eyes stung so much that they felt as big as oranges, yet for the first time in her life it was as if she could see her insides too—the rawness of her heart, struggling to pump blood round a body that wanted only to feel Ryan's heart beating against it, and the lethargy of limbs so addicted to being entwined with muscled masculine ones that they were incapable of functioning solo. And even though the knowledge that Ryan was gone from her life was as tangible and uncomfortable as a cold, damp blanket wrapped around her, it couldn't entirely douse the tiny pathetic flame of hope that he'd come back…that he'd realise they belonged together…that…

The sound of the brass knocker on the front door sent her thoughts flying away. *Ryan!*

'Ryan!' she shouted, racing wildly for the foyer. 'Oh, Ryan!' she gasped, half laughing, half crying as she fumbled to open the front door. 'Oh, Ryan, I knew you'd come—' Her words and the joy spontaneously aborted at the sight of a stranger in grease-stained overalls staring hesitantly at her.

'Er, are you Ms Cosgrove?'

Over his right shoulder she spotted a shiny maroon van with LANE'S AUTO TUNE emblazoned in the door, only subconsciously noting another man sitting behind the wheel as dread flooded her.

'Oh, God, he's had an accident!'

'No! No!' the man said, pulling back from the grasp she had on his shoulders. 'There isn't an accident.'

'Ry-Ryan's OK?'

'Was when he left the Jag at the garage.' Smiling, he dangled a set of keys in her face. 'He asked me to drop the car back to you.'

She glanced at the keys, then stepped past the man onto the front veranda and saw Ryan's Jag parked behind the maroon car.

'He left his car for me to drive?'

'Yeah. Said you might need it and didn't want to leave

you stranded. Half your luck! I don't usually do the delivery of cars, but I sure wasn't about to pass up a chance to drive that beauty!' The man gave a hearty chuckle. 'He said *I'd* be doing *him* a favour.'

Kirrily simply stared at the car, her lack of enthusiasm obviously puzzling the mechanic.

'So...er...would you like me to put it into the garage for you?'

'What I'd like would be for you to put it into the *wall* of the garage,' she said through gritted teeth. 'But then it'll be so much more fun to do it myself!'

The man's appalled gasp snapped her from her vindictive thoughts. She drew a breath and forced a smile.

'I'm sorry...' she glanced at the name embroidered on his overalls '...Dan, I didn't mean that. It's just I'm amazed Ryan would've left me his car. I thought he was driving to Sydney.'

'Told me he was hiring another. You oughta be happy, though—you got the best end of the deal; there's no way he could've hired anything that swish around here. Lucky you get to travel in style.'

'Yeah,' she said. 'I'm just born lucky and happy beyond my wildest dreams.' She closed her fist round the keys, knowing that no one who'd heard her deliver that line would have believed she made a living from acting.

'Hi, Kirri—'

'Kirrily! What are you—?'

'Kirrily, what's—?'

Rage drove her—week-old, white-hot, blistering rage that swept her past the startled faces of assorted Talbot's employees and customers.

She deserved better! She deserved a hell of a lot better! A hell of a lot more than he'd given her—which was *nothing*! Ignoring the hesitant cautions which followed her, she grabbed the handle of his office door and stormed through it.

Ryan's head jerked up in reaction to the slam of his office door and shock paralysed him. Face flushed, eyes hard as emeralds, hair in windswept disarray she looked more exquisite than the image woven into his tormented memory.

'There!' she said, tossing his Jaguar keys on his desk so hard that they bounced. 'And now you owe me an explanation!' Her anger was as potent as the tidal wave of desire rushing through him. 'I'm not the type who takes getting screwed and dumped in silence, Ryan Talbot!'

'For God's sake, keep your voice down! You want the whole office to hear?'

'Nor do I take it quietly!' she screamed even louder. 'I don't care who hears it!'

'Damn it, K.C., calm—'

'I will not calm down! I don't want to calm down! Don't you *dare* tell me what to do, you…you…'

Her momentary confusion gave Ryan the chance to skirt the desk and grab hold of her flailing arms.

'Let me go!' she screeched. 'Let me go, you bast—'

'Not yet! I want you to settle down.'

She went instantly still.

'Settle down?' she echoed. *'Settle down!'* Her laugh was bitter with irony. 'Oh, that's rich! That's really, really precious! A week ago I was praying for you to tell me you wanted me to settle down…settle down with *you*—permanently—have your kids, spend the re—'

Her voice broke from the sheer overpowering effect of his nearness; his scent, his body warmth, the gentle yet firm pressure of his hands around her upper arms all conspired against her. Kirrily knew then she'd made a mistake. She should never have come—should never have seen him again, never put herself into the position she was in now, where his softly crooned platitudes whispered across the top of her head and sensitised her all the way to her toes and made her tremble.

'It's OK, honey… It's OK…'

She shook her head, without lifting it from his chest. It wasn't OK. Despite how good, how energised, how hopeful being this close to him made her feel, she knew it wasn't OK. He was as far beyond her reach as Steven was from Jayne, but unlike Jayne she couldn't allow her life to become an ongoing valediction to lost love. If she was to survive, much less salvage any part of her former self, she needed to believe that this mistake had been Ryan's, not hers; she wanted no reason to exonerate him.

Inhaling hard, as if determination were drawn from oxygen, she tried to ease out of his hold. He resisted.

'Kirrily, I can explain—'

'No!' She pushed hard at his chest, freeing herself. 'I don't want an explanation. I thought I did, but I don't.'

'Kirrily, listen—'

'No. No, I won't listen. Our history proves that whenever we've disagreed about something you've invariably been right. If I listen to your explanation it'll happen again. I know you'll have a feasible reason why you said you loved me then a few days later walked away. Well, I don't want you to be in the right this time, Ryan.'

She paused, taking another deep breath before continuing. 'If you're right about this, I'll never have a reason to hate you. And I want to hate you, Ryan.' The pain burning at her heart brought tears to her eyes. She ignored them. 'I want to hate you for making me love you. I want to hate you for giving me the most wonderful six days of my life and spoiling me for any other male who may fall in love with me.'

When he flinched, she shook her head. 'I'm not talking about my virginity, Ryan. I *chose* to give you that and…and, well, these days guys expect *not* to be the first, just as they can accept being offered a bruised, battered heart. But I can't even offer that now, because you didn't just leave my heart bruised and battered,

Ryan, you ripped it clear out of my chest; I'll never be able to return another man's love even if I want to.'

Paralysis shut down Ryan's emotional, physical and mental faculties to the extent that he could do nothing more than stare at her.

'Goodbye, Ryan.'

Her expression and tone were chillingly final as she turned from him and she'd gripped the handle of the door before he could force any words past the emotion wedged in his throat.

'Kirrily, wait!'

She stopped, but didn't turn around.

'I can give you a reason to hate me… I'm responsible for Steven's death. It's *my* fault your brother is dead.'

CHAPTER FOURTEEN

SHOCKED senseless by the enormity of the words, Kirrily braced both hands against the door to steady herself. For long, endless moments all she heard above the silence of the room was her pounding heart. Then her brain began chanting... *Lie! Lie! Lie!*

'Steven was killed because a drunk ran a give way sign.' The strain in her voice gave the statement a breathless uncertainty that she immediately tried to dispel. '*I know* that's the truth. *I know it is!*'

Defeating the dull, numb sensation in her limbs, she turned to face him, her heart tearing at the anguish clouding Ryan's eyes.

'I've always suspected I didn't know everything,' she said. 'But I *do* know Steve isn't dead because of anything you did.'

'He should never have been driving...*I* should have. We'd been at the pub and...'

He turned from her silent plea for explanation, leaving her mentally fumbling to understand what he was telling her.

'Are...are you saying Steve was drunk at the wheel?'

'Hell, no!' He swung back to her, looking horrified, then lowered his head for only a heartbeat before once more aligning his gaze with hers. '*I* was the one who was drunk!'

'You mean...y-y-you were driving?'

'I should've been. It was my turn...' His voice had a far-away quality suggesting he was being distracted by memories of long-ago. 'My recklessness, my "to hell with responsibility" attitude killed Steve as surely as if I'd been behind the wheel of the other car. *I* was supposed to be driving that night, dammit!'

The more he spoke, the less Kirrily understood, and frustration began dispersing the fog of apprehension his claim had initially evoked.

'I don't understand any of this...' She moved closer, as if expecting that lessening the distance separating them would make things clearer; Ryan took a matching number of steps back.

'Dammit, Ryan, stand still! This isn't making any sense—*you're* not making any sense!' she accused him, flailing her arms in helplessness. 'In one breath you're saying *you* should have been driving and in the next breath you're saying *you* were drunk, yet I don't think I've ever seen you have more than two drinks on the same day in my life, and as for the *other*—huh!' Her face matched the scepticism of her tone. 'You're the *least* reckless, *most* responsible person I've ever known.'

'You're confusing me with your brother.'

Kirrily's reply was pungently explicit, then she said, 'I could never confuse you with anybody!' She sighed, her voice and expression softening. 'How could I? I only have to *think* of you for my heart to start hammering and my insides to mush up; no other human being has ever had that effect on me... No other ever will.'

Ryan clenched his fists at his sides to stop himself from hauling her into his arms and responding to the love shining from her thick-lashed eyes. He couldn't allow himself to be moved by her words and feelings until he was sure she understood what he was telling her. As the silence lengthened between them, Ryan felt the consequences of what he was about to say as an almost unendurable physical weight. Sighing, he crossed to his chair and sank into it.

'What do you remember about Steven?' he asked at

length, noting she'd instinctively opened her mouth to protest at the question then changed her mind. She glanced at the chair across the desk from his, seemingly surprised that it was there, then gingerly lowered herself onto it, as if suspecting that it might buck her off.

'Sometimes it's hard to picture him,' she said in little more than a whisper. 'I know he was really good-looking, that you and he were called the "heartbreak twins" and that even though every girl in the neighbourhood was chasing him he was crazy about Jayne.' A faint smile touched her lips. 'When he couldn't go out with her because he got stuck babysitting me he'd tell me I was a pest and that when he and Jayne got married they'd have a dozen kids, just so babysitting could wreck my social life the way I wrecked his—'

The teary shine in her eyes prompted Ryan to interrupt. 'He didn't really think you a pest, K.C.—he adored you.'

'Oh, I know he was teasing,' she said quickly. 'He was always so...so kind, so funny, so...'

'*Responsible.*'

Hearing Ryan say the word so resentfully jolted her from her melancholy. 'Well...yes,' she said, recalling how everyone had commented about how 'that Cosgrove boy's got his head screwed on nice and tight'.

'Yes,' she said again. 'You and Steve are... *were*...alike in that respect.'

'No.' The word was hard. 'We weren't.'

'But you're—'

'What do you remember about me as a kid, Kirrily?'

She frowned, considering the question. 'I remember you helping me with my homework, the way Steve used to. And driving me to netball training when Mum and Dad couldn't take me, and—'

'Before all that,' he cut in. 'What do you remember about me *before* Steven was killed?'

It surprised her to find that she had to struggle for a

clear memory. 'Er…I remember you blacking out the street on Christmas Eve…' She bit her lip. 'Well, I don't *remember* it exactly, but I remember everyone talking about it.'

'And…' he prompted.

'And I remember Dad taking me to watch you and Steve play football and one time you getting sent off for starting a brawl.' A slow grin spread across her face. 'Boy, was your dad ever ticked off about that! Almost as much as when you got suspended for sneaking booze into a school dance.'

'Hardly the stuff of a responsible kid, eh, K.C.?'

'Well, no…but kids do that sort of thing—'

'Ever hear of Steve doing it?' he challenged.

'No, but I know he was usually with you—'

'Yeah, he was there all right,' Ryan agreed. 'Sometimes trying to talk me out of getting into strife, but mostly hauling me out of it or trying to cover my butt.' He shook his head, his eyes distant and sad. 'Steve was the responsible one, not me. We were as different as chalk and cheese, yet he understood me better than anyone else.' His eyes again sparked to life. 'It was him who convinced my dad that my going to uni and studying architecture wasn't a sell-out.'

The implication confused Kirrily. 'But Bob's so proud of you…I can't believe he didn't want you to go to university.'

'Believe it. From the time Steve and I began spending our school vacations working on building sites our dads had everything mapped out: we'd finish school, serve our carpentry apprenticeships with each other's father, get our building licences and from there it would only be a matter of time before the folks retired and we took over running Talbot's. The whole scenario was a *fait accompli* until I threw a spanner in the works with what Dad called my ''highfalutin ideas''.'

Kirrily knew only too well that, in the eyes of most

hands-on builders, architects were glorified draftsmen who considered the dirt and grime of a building site below them. Not only that; often their sad lack of knowledge regarding the practicalities of building saw their grandiose plans and theories run way beyond budget and scheduled completion time. Knowing how scathing Bob Talbot could be about architects, even now that his son was one, Kirrily imagined that back then Ryan's decision would have amounted to treason in his eyes.

'Things were pretty tense between Dad and me for a while there,' Ryan continued as he twisted a pen between his fingers. 'But somehow Steve convinced the old man it'd be to the firm's advantage to have an architect who understood the hands-on realities of the building game rather than simply the ivory-tower theories. Eventually he grudgingly agreed to pay my way through uni.'

'What would you have done if he hadn't agreed?'

'Left home.'

'And what?' she asked, a little surprised at how certain his response had been. 'Worked as a labourer during the day and put yourself through uni at night?'

He smiled ruefully. 'I doubt it. I wasn't the type to take on that much responsibility or that much hard work. Which was why university appealed to me: a light schedule of lectures and tutorials during the day, a heavy schedule of parties during the night.' There was no hint of remorse or apology in either his tone or expression.

'I don't believe you,' she said flatly.

He shrugged. 'It's the truth.'

'*Really?* So what saint is credited with the miracle of turning you from a layabout student and premier party animal to the highest passing graduate in your year and *my* self-appointed morality warden?'

Her tone was only a breath away from being downright scathing, but Ryan found her choice of words

ironic; over the years he'd often felt he was trying to fill
the shoes of a saint.

'Not a miracle,' he said, his voice rough. 'A tragedy.
A tragedy that could have been avoided, if I hadn't been
so obsessed with always having a good time.'

He paused, but Kirrily resisted the urge to prompt
him; instead she collated what she could remember from
that night years ago.

It had been a tradition that both the Cosgroves and
Talbots spent every Easter break at a caravan park in the
south coast town of Ulladulla. At nine, Kirrily's excur-
sions into the town had been accompanied and curfewed,
so while Steven, Ryan and Jayne had thrown themselves
into the local social scene *her* evenings had been spent
with her parents and the Talbots, playing either cards or
board games. The night Steven died had started out as
no different than any other one that Easter, she thought.

It suddenly dawned on her that Ryan had resumed
speaking; though she'd missed his first few words the
pain in his voice stopped her from asking him to repeat
himself.

'I don't know what they'd had the tiff over, but Jayne
was sulking and Steve couldn't talk her into coming to
the pub with us,' he said. 'We had an arrangement—
whenever the three of us went out together we'd take
turns driving. It was Jayne's turn that night, but since
Steve had driven the previous night and Jayne wasn't
going I was the designated driver.' He paused, rubbing
his eyes with his thumb and forefinger. 'I had the dirts
because I figured since it was Steve's girl who'd stuffed
up the roster *he* ought to be the reserve driver, but he
just grinned and tossed me the keys, saying, ''Yeah,
mate, but she's *your* sister!''

'I'd more or less accepted the injustice of it all until
it became painfully obvious the hot blonde I was putting
the moves on at the pub was more interested in Steve.

Steve! Who was so damn crazy about my sister he couldn't even *see* he was cramping my style!'

Kirrily could only assume that her brother must have been *way* better looking than she remembered or else the blonde had been blind.

'Anyway, the more of a battering my ego took, the more I drank. I was a long way from being plastered, but by the time the blonde's ex-boyfriend turned up and started giving her a hard time I was more than ready to lay down my life to get her to notice me. To this day all I remember is landing the first punch and then...and then waking up in an overturned car and smelling petrol and burning rubber.'

'That,' he said, 'and watching Steven and the hopes of everyone who loved him die in my arms. He'd hauled me unconscious from a pub brawl and saved my butt, but I couldn't save his life.'

'Oh, God...'

Though she'd known Ryan had pulled Steven from the smouldering wreck, holding him until he'd died, Kirrily had never stopped to consider the impact the event had had on his life. While her parents' and Jayne's grief had been highly visible and touched everyone she'd simply assumed that Ryan had survived the ordeal relatively unscathed. She'd been wrong.

Her gaze followed him as he rose and walked to the one-way glass window overlooking the company's loading bay. The fabric of his shirt stretched across his wide, strong shoulders, yet how much stronger must his heart have been to have carried the weight of his guilt for more than a dozen years? For in that instant she realised that not only had Ryan assumed the guilt for what had happened but he'd also assumed the responsibilities that would have fallen to Steven had he lived: Jayne, the family business...*her*.

'He was conscious the whole time I was trying to get him out—kept telling me the car was gonna blow and

to get the hell away. I managed to get him clear of the
car; it didn't explode but, God, the smell! I'll never forget that stench.'

When he breathed deeply, as if embracing the purity
of the air in his office, she had to force herself not to go
to him and wrap her arms around him—not because she
needed to hear what he'd been through, but because she
sensed he needed to talk it out.

'People were starting to come out of their houses; I
could hear sirens in the distance. I told Steve to hang in
there, that the ambulance was on its way. "Good," he
said. "'Cos you sure look like you need one, Talbot."
He was so lucid, I figured he wasn't hurt as badly as I'd
thought. Even when he asked me to tell Jayne that he
was sorry they'd fought and that he loved her, I told him
he could do it himself, that I wasn't going to sort out
his romantic squabbles. And then he mentioned you...'

'M-m-me?' Her voice was choked and Ryan spoke
over the top of it.

'He said that though it'd probably be a case of the
blind leading the blind he'd really appreciate it if I could
watch out for you while you were growing up. "Keep
an eye on her, for me, mate," he said. "I reckon K.C.
is going to be more than my folks can handle on their
own." Then he winked at me and said, "And Ry, mate,
you've gotta stop being such a damn sucker for
blondes."'

'I thought, Hey, if he's cracking jokes, he *must* be
OK. That he was...you know...in better shape than he
looked... But he wasn't...' His shoulder lifted as he
heaved an audible breath, then he turned back to her, his
face contorted with the strain of reliving the past. 'He
was dead before the ambulance arrived.'

'Oh, Ryan...'

The sob-strangled sound of his name and the tears
coursing unchecked down her perfect face filled Ryan
with a pain like none he'd ever imagined. His first in-

stinct as she dropped her face into her hands was to take
her in his arms and absorb every bit of her pain, but the
sheer futility of such an action kept him immobile across
the room. He was the last person to console her because
her knowing what she now did meant that his very existence would only intensify her suffering. Still, the sight
and sound of her sorrow ripped at the very core of Ryan
and it seemed an eternity before her distress decreased
from heart-rending sobs to weak, muffled hiccups.

It was still some time before she lifted her head to
look at him. 'So that's what everyone's been keeping
from me all these years.' The detached calmness in her
voice both surprised and worried him; surely rage, sarcasm or blame would have been more normal reactions?
His concern grew as she got to her feet and started
straightening things on his desk, her actions agitated despite her efforts to appear casual.

'Does Jayne know?' she asked, not looking at him.

'Yes.'

'But *she* still blamed herself for what happened?'

'It wasn't her fault, Kirrily...'

'I know that.' Her gaze met his with steady directness.
'But it wasn't yours either, Ryan.'

'I was supposed to be driv—'

'No!' Her denial was swift and tempered. 'Jayne
thinks *she* should have been driving; you said it yourself—it was *her* turn.'

'Stop it now, Kirrily. Shifting the blame to Jayne
won't bring Steven back.'

'Of course it won't!' she agreed. 'Damn it, Ryan, I'm
not trying to blame Jayne. Why would I when she's
spent the last fifteen years punishing herself? The same
as *you* have!'

'You're talking rubbish—'

'Bull! What the hell is it with you Talbots that you
all want to turn yourself into whipping boys? Jayne was
so desperate to atone for her imagined guilt and keep

the memory of Steven alive that she had a phantom pregnancy and then became an emotional recluse. And *you*—
you, Ryan—' she rounded the desk moving towards him
'—you tried to turn yourself into him!'

'Like I said, you're talking rubbish.'

'Am I? Then why did you turn your back on the junior
partnership at one of the most successful architecture
firms in the country to run Talbot's when your father
retired?'

'It was always expected that I'd take over—'

'No, it was always expected that *Steven* would take
over! Just as it was always expected that Steven would
be there to look after Jayne and be a big brother to me.
No one was more stunned than our parents when you
announced you wanted to take over Talbot's. I remember
our dads saying they'd give you two years, *tops*, before
you'd be champing at the bit to get back to what you
loved best...*architecture*!'

'Then they were wrong, weren't they?'

'No, dammit, they weren't wrong! You *hate* what
you're doing! Don't deny it!' she exploded when he
opened his mouth as if he was going to. 'I've seen the
hundreds of designs you've got buried away down at the
house. I spent the better part of a week studying them
and...'

'And what?'

'And they're *good*. Excellent, in fact.'

'You're an actor, Kirrily; you don't know enough
about architecture to give your judgement credibility.'

'Maybe not, but I know *you*. And every one of those
plans explains and reflects a lot about you, Ryan.'

'Cut the bull, Kirrily. They're nothing more than
drawings.'

She shook her head. 'They're your dreams, Ryan.'

His laugh was harsh. 'If they are, then they're pipe-
dreams.'

'But don't you see? They don't have to stay that way.

You're a brilliant architect; you could probably sell them all tomorrow if you tried. But you won't,' she said. 'Because that's not what you really want, is it?'

'You tell me; you seem to have it all figured out.'

'Yeah,' she said smugly. 'I do. You'll never sell those drawings because you couldn't stand the thought of your concepts being butchered by someone who doesn't really care about them, someone who's only interested in making a quick buck. You aren't from the "draw a pretty house and let someone else do the work" school of design, you're a hands-on, "get in there and sweat it out" architect—one who wants the cement dust on his clothes and the splinters in his hands.' She paused only long enough to give him a knowing smile. 'If ever you decided to build those houses to sell you'd put every bit as much effort, care and commitment into each one as you did the one at Bowral.'

'Which wouldn't make a financially sound business venture since I haven't had the time to finish the only one I've started,' he said. 'Nothing you've said is practical. Sure, I was hands-on with the house at Bowral, but only because it was a personal investment.'

'Building it was *emotional therapy*, pure and simple,' she countered. 'Because the frustration of doing a job you yourself said could be handled by any half-decent builder was driving you crazy.'

'Believe what you will, Kirrily; it doesn't alter the fact that fifteen years ago my selfishness not only caused Steven's death but a lot of deep, irrevocable pain to the people who most cared about him and me. I swore nothing like that would ever happen again and I've made it a rule not to do anything where I run the risk of letting those people down again. I've got responsibilities—to our parents, to Jayne, to—'

'Shut up about your dumb rules and your responsibilities to everyone else!' she ordered. 'What about your responsibilities to yourself, to your own happiness? Like you said, the pain is *irrevocable*—nothing you do or don't do can change it. This might come as a shock, Ryan, but you're not God, you can't be certain the accident wouldn't have happened or would have turned out differently had you been at the wheel. Well?' she pressed. 'Can you?'

'No, dammit, I can't! But I do know the circumstances of Steve's death are always going to be between us, and sooner or later you'll end up hating me because of it.'

The pain in his face and voice nearly crippled her heart, but the way he shrugged away from her when she tried to comfort him was far more debilitating.

'Just leave, Kirrily. Your forgiveness only makes the guilt harder to bear.'

'My hatred would be easier to handle, is that it?' She answered her own question before he had a chance, her tone deliberately goading. 'Yeah,' she said. 'I guess it would be since you've had so much experience dealing with it; after all, you've been hating and punishing yourself for years.'

Kirrily knew she was treading dangerously, but she hoped that in anger Ryan would admit what she so desperately needed to hear. 'For years you've assumed the role of not just a protector to all but that of a martyr too, by denying yourself your dreams and ambitions. And now...well, now you've taken it to new heights; you're denying yourself love. *My* love.'

His impassive expression infuriated her. 'Damn it, Ryan!' she said hotly. 'Admit it, why don't you?'

When he stubbornly remained mute Kirrily knew there was nothing more she could do or say. Swearing at the tears again blurring her vision, she snatched his car keys off the desk and, storming to the door, pulled it open. It might have been only a last tenacious smidgen of hope that made her stop and turn to him one more time, but if so the remoteness in his eyes squashed it.

'I've done some dumb things in my life, but falling

for you, Ryan Talbot, takes the prize! But I will not—repeat, *will not*—give you the satisfaction of hating you! I…I hope you choke on your stupid rules and…and your precious responsibilities and misplaced guilt!'

The slam of the door on her exit was far louder than the one that had announced her entrance.

CHAPTER FIFTEEN

RYAN sat at his desk feeling as if he was in an emotional
wind-tunnel being buffeted against one wall then the
other, ricocheting back and forth between a sense of
overwhelming relief that he'd finally unburdened himself
and the terminal despair of knowing he'd driven Kirrily
from his life.

At first he'd kept the truth from her because Steve had
wanted him to take care of her, and he'd feared she'd
have hated him too much to enable him to honour his
promise to his best friend. Later...well, he'd simply told
himself he was waiting for the right time, yet somehow
the time had never been quite right. He'd found dozens
of reasons to justify his ongoing silence: Kirrily was
Jayne's sole confidant—how would his emotionally
fragile sister cope if learning the truth turned Kirrily
against her? Or what if Kirrily's own despair caused her
to withdraw from life as Jayne had done?

Oh, he'd had countless excuses to draw on, and he
had drawn on them, but the reality was that over the
years he'd gone from being a well-intentioned but naïve
twenty-one-year-old to being a selfish, self-deluding idiot! He'd refused to consciously acknowledge that
Kirrily had developed from a tiny waif-like nine-year-
old, whom he was supposed to guide, into a beautiful,
sensual, intelligent woman who knew her own mind.

But his subconscious and his heart had been more
astute, had known that what he was trying to persuade

himself as only hormonal lust was actually the big L. *Love*. The "til death do us part' variety.

And it had been he who'd let death part them. A fifteen-year-old death.

He'd sworn that if he ever truly fell in love with a woman he'd tell her the truth about what had happened and that if she loved him she'd understand and forgive him.

Kirrily had understood.

Kirrily had understood *better* and *more* than anybody.

Better than even he had.

She'd said there was *nothing* to forgive. That she wouldn't hate him but that falling for him was the dumbest thing she'd ever done—hell, it probably was! he thought. But the dumbest thing he could ever do was let her out of his life!

'Where are my keys?' he bellowed, shoving files from his desk. 'She threw them right—' Damn, she had his car! No problem, he decided, hurrying to the door; he'd take the company van and—

He collided with a mass of male muscle.

'Dammit, Nichols!' he snapped, pushing past the man in the doorway. 'What do you want?'

'I came to discuss the plumbing stuff on that duplex I'm tendering for, but, judging by the way a certain young lady stormed out of your office not long ago, I guess now isn't a good time, huh?'

'You've got that right!' Ryan rummaged around the desk of his senior sales rep. 'Julie,' he called, ignoring the amused Trevor Nichols. 'Where the devil are the keys for the ute?'

His receptionist frowned. 'At the mechanics, I guess, *with the ute*. It's getting a new starter motor... remember?'

Ryan's expletive should have peeled the paint from the walls, but it merely drew hearty laughter from Trevor Nichols. Overdosing on frustration, Ryan was mentally gauging how much of it would be released if he decked the guy on the spot, when a bundle of keys was jiggled under his nose.

'Take my car, Talbot—the red Bronco in the parking lot. I can get one of my apprentices to pick me up.'

Surprise only momentarily slowed Ryan's reaction, then, grinning, he grabbed the keys and bolted for the door. 'Thanks, mate,' he called to Nichols over his shoulder. 'I owe you one!'

'Just invite me to the wedding so I can kiss the bride without ending up with a broken nose like Rick!'

Ryan was in too much of a hurry to tell Nichols not to rely on tradition to protect his good looks!

As he drove past the sign indicating that he was entering the Central Coast suburb of Avoca, where Kirrily's parents now lived, Ryan's heart started pumping faster.

She had to be here! She *had* to! It was almost eight hours since he'd taken off after her and he was running out of places to look.

When he'd left the office he'd made the short trip to his Cabarita house, expecting to find her packing, but either he'd just missed her or she'd packed before coming to see him, because there were no signs that she'd ever been there. Worried she might have elected to return immediately to Melbourne, he'd checked at the airport to see if she'd booked a flight, relief flooding him when there'd been no sign of his car in the car park. Then, figuring she must have driven back to Bowral, he'd headed towards the Southern Tablelands at speed, earning himself a speeding ticket before even clearing the outer limits of Sydney. But when he had finally entered the house he'd left a week ago he'd known the sense of emptiness he experienced had nothing to do with the lack of furnishings; Kirrily wasn't there.

With hindsight he'd realised it was stupid to think she'd choose to hide somewhere that belonged to him;

had he been thinking rationally, her parents' home would
have been the first place he'd have looked. Of course,
he hadn't been thinking all that rationally today.

Today? Hell, he hadn't been thinking too rationally
for the best part of fifteen years! Dammit, she had to be
here! *She simply had to!*

The crash and tinkle of crushing metal and glass had
Kirrily pressing her forehead against the bay window
and scanning the darkened front yard and driveway.

'Oh, no!' she wailed, her eyes settling on the image
of a large vehicle with its front end pressed hard against
the rear of Ryan's Jag. 'I don't believe this!'

Praying she was hallucinating, she hurried to the front
door, barely remembering to punch in the security code
before opening it.

'Please let me be imagining this,' she muttered, stepping with closed eyes out onto the veranda. 'Dear God,'
she prayed aloud, 'when I open my eyes let me not discover Trev Nichols has rear-ended Ryan's beautiful
car...'

She opened her eyes and found that God was on a
coffee-break.

'Aagh!' she screamed. 'Trevor, you bloody idiot, what
have you *done*?'

'It's not Trevor who's the idiot—it's me.'

The voice from below almost caused her to topple
over the railing of the elevated veranda.

'R-*Ryan!* What...? How...?' She knew she sounded
incoherent, but at least that was consistent with how she
felt. She glanced back at the red four by four, the muted
glow of the entrance light sufficient to confirm that it
was empty, then back to Ryan, who was climbing the
steps to her left.

Her pulse-rate was manic in a combination of fright,
fear and an overwhelming relief that he didn't appear
hurt. Actually he didn't even seemed fazed that he'd

driven a mean-looking bull-bar into the backside of an expensive luxury car. *His* expensive luxury car.

'I guess I wasn't firm enough on the brakes,' he said, halting only an arm's length from her. 'You know…not used to the car.'

'What…what…are—?' Kirrily shook her head and started again. 'What are you doing here with Trevor's car?'

'You mean besides playing demolition derby in your folks' driveway?'

'*Ryan!* How can you joke about doing that much damage to—?' Her voice stalled when two large but gentle hands cupped her face and angled her head until it was only inches from his own. Completely transfixed by the man holding her, she felt rather than heard his hoarse whisper of her name.

'What I've done to the cars only requires cash to repair it. I'm more worried about the damage I've done to *us*, to our future.'

The emotion in his voice and the reverent caresses of his thumbs over her cheekbones as he studied her face filled Kirrily with what she could only call spiritual warmth.

'I love you, Kirrily. I love you more than I'll ever be able to tell you or even show you. You're more precious to me than my own life and I'm sorrier than you'll ever know for what I've put you through. I'm a fool for—'

'Shh.' She covered his mouth with her fingers. 'You're not a fool, Ryan Talbot.' She smiled, absently tracing his mouth and jaw. 'The proof being I'm way too smart to fall in love with a fool and I definitely fell for you *big time*.'

'Only hours ago you said that was the dumbest thing you ever did.'

'I said a lot of things I had no right to say.'

'Yes, you did, because everything you said was true. My life *has* been controlled by guilt. Logically I know the accident was just that, an *accident*, but I can't help wondering if—'

He swore softly, before burying his face in her hair, and instinctively Kirrily nestled closer, tightening her arms around him to convey her understanding, her trust and her love. She knew there was a lot Ryan still needed to work through, that he couldn't simply shrug himself free of the past because he wanted to, but at least now he believed it wasn't wrong to try.

When he finally lifted his head his expression told her he'd heard everything that had been in her heart.

'I don't just love you, Kirrily,' he said, his voice rough with emotion, 'I *need* you. I need you to make me whole again, to help me get my life back in order. I need you *in my life*, on a daily basis.'

The sound of love was behind every one of his words, seemingly giving wings to her heart, yet she ached to erase the too humble expression on his handsome face. How could he ever think she'd turn him down? She reached up and caressed his puckered brow. 'Oh?' she said, determined to goad him back to normality. 'Does that mean you're offering me a permanent position in Talbot's accounts department?'

'*What?*' He looked completely poleaxed and, struggling to contain her amusement, Kirrily continued.

'Well,' she mused aloud, 'I could certainly use a job—'

'Damn it, Kirrily!' he snapped, giving her shoulders a quick, sharp shake. 'I'm not talking about Talbot's! I'm *proposing* and you know it!'

The joy flooding her system was prompted as much by his adorable exasperation as by the words themselves. 'Oh!' she said with pseudo-shock. 'I guess I just always assumed the guy who asked me to marry him would at least *smile* as he did it. *Not*,' she added quickly, linking her arms around his neck, 'that a smile is essential for getting an affirmative response from me.'

The return of genuine amusement to his blue eyes made her chuckle.

'Does that,' he asked, rubbing her nose with his, 'mean yes?'

Easing some space between them, she adopted a considering look. 'Does a yes mean I'd get to set a few of the rules in our marriage?'

He groaned and tugged her back against him. 'That depends,' he muttered against her neck, 'on how many I'd have to keep.'

'Only one,' she whispered, rising onto her toes to be closer to his warmth.

'And that would be?'

She lifted her eyes to his. 'That you love me for ever...'

'I already have,' he groaned, lowering his head to hers.

The myriad emotions that Ryan's kiss inspired within her were beyond anything Kirrily could have imagined, much less described. It was as if everything she'd ever felt from him or for him—warmth ... friendship ... desire ... irritation ... amusement ... frustration ... tranquillity ... excitement ... tenderness ... passion—had all blended in a huge melting pot until the only element strong enough to retain its true identity was love. A love so powerful that every aspect of her existence was now flavoured with it. Almost limp with the need to experience again her lover's total possession of her, Kirrily murmured a grateful sigh as she was swung into his strong arms and carried into the house.

Ryan's good intention of getting to Kirrily's bedroom before he lost all control went to hell in a basket the moment the woman in his arms set her frantic tongue loose at the base of his throat. In the wake of its eager, slickly seductive journey along the column of his neck and across his jaw, it was all he could manage to heel the front door closed and slump against it, before lowering her to the floor.

The feel of her body sliding the length of his was painfully erotic. In his desire-drugged state he saw the solution being to draw her tighter against his arousal, a guttural groan breaking from him as simultaneously Kirrily, too, pressed for greater contact rather than distance. With one hand he clamped her hips to his as the other grasped her hair and dragged her delectably sweet mouth back to his. Her response was instant, ardent and heated.

Ryan's kiss swirled through Kirrily at the speed of light, igniting her blood and blurring her mind to everything but him, until she was barely aware of their muted moans, her desperate gasps for air and Ryan's chanted endearments. She wanted to tell him such verbalising was redundant because she could *feel* love emanating from him, but words were beyond her, her body keyed only to the senses of taste and touch. The touch of Ryan. The taste of Ryan.

The contact of his hands against her bare skin as they slipped beneath the hem of her sweatshirt had her own feverishly joining in to help wrench it off. Within seconds their unspoken co-operation resulted in their lying naked in the carpeted hallway of her parents' home.

'You're the most beautiful thing I've ever seen.' Ryan's voice was raspy as he looked down at her, his eyes bright with adoration. 'So goddamn beautiful,' he muttered, lowering his head.

The muscles in her belly contracted and she moaned with pleasure as his lips laved the aroused peak of one breast, then the other, the sensations he triggered all the more incredible because she knew they were spawned from their unique love—a love that had grown as they'd grown but that would stay young even as they aged, a love that because it had no clear beginning could have no end.

Ryan's tongue had moved down to probe and tantalise the depth of her navel and Kirrily's anticipation began contributing, with his slow oral assault, to draw her closer and closer to screaming point. In her ears all she heard was the rhythm of her pounding heart and her own ragged breathing, as both her body and soul cried for complete reunion with his.

'Easy,' he crooned as she bucked beneath him, her hands tightening in his hair. 'Ea...sy.'

'No!' Hands urgent, she pulled at his hair, the action raising his head just far enough to make eye contact with her. 'I need you *now*, Ryan,' she whispered, her hands gentling. '*All* of you.'

The emotion in her voice and the emerald depths of her eyes gave her words the sentiments of a prayer rather than a plea and Ryan was incapable of denying it. Their gazes locked, he repositioned himself above her. Automatically he reached for his jeans, hastily extracting his wallet, but Kirrily snatched it away.

'Uh-uh,' she said. 'I just want you, Ryan. *No barriers*—not the past, not even a condom. Just you, me, the future and *whatever* it holds for us.'

With a groan he accepted her ready warmth, knowing this woman's love was his personal salvation.

EPILOGUE

'JAYNE'S here,' Kirrily noted, looking from the kitchen to the pool area where both her parents and in-laws were welcoming the late arrival. Ryan joined her at the window.

'Aw, hell,' he muttered. 'She's still got Trevor Nichols in tow.'

Kirrily gave her husband of four months a frown. 'I thought you liked Trevor?'

'I do. I just don't like him panting after my sister. He's too experienced for her. Heck, he's married with four kids—'

'*Divorced*—' both Kirrily and Ryan spun in the direction of the intruding voice '—with three,' corrected Jayne, wearing an amused grin at her brother's sheepish expression. 'And don't worry about him *panting* after me, big brother,' she said, standing on her toes to reach Ryan's cheek. 'I'm more than capable of bringing him to heel.'

Kirrily laughed and hugged her sister-in-law. 'Ignore him and date whoever makes you happy,' she advised.

'Are you happy, sis?' Ryan asked gently.

'Yeah.' A light blush rose on his sister's cheeks as she glanced outside. 'Very.'

Ryan grinned. 'Then I guess I'd better go give Nichols a beer.' Slipping his arm around his sister's shoulders, he steered her towards the glass doors leading to the patio. 'But he makes one more crack about my driving ability and he'll wear it!' he warned.

Kirrily watched from the window as Ryan warmly welcomed the only man Jayne had shown any interest in since Steven's death. The presence of Trevor's three teenage children seemed to indicate that their relationship was more than casual. Good, she thought, wanting her sister-in-law to be every bit as happy as she was, although seriously doubting that was possible. The last six months of her life had been more than she could have dreamed of...

Within weeks of their parents arriving back from Europe they'd married and set up residence at Bowral. Eager to re-establish himself as an architect, Ryan had eased himself out of Talbot's, restricting his involvement to simply a consulting basis and leaving the day-to-day running of the place to Ron Flemming.

Already a house he'd designed and supervised the building of for a prominent musician was nearing completion, and he was being inundated with requests for future projects. Currently he was working out of the den at home, but at this rate they were going to have to build a bigger, separate office away from the house, if only to guarantee professional credibility; with them both at home, all too often they confused the boardroom with the bedroom!

Though Kirrily had secured only a two-episode part in a Sydney-based drama, she was kept busy with voice-overs for radio and television commercials and the small interior-design business Ryan had encouraged her to start. To date she'd only done a couple of small redecorating projects for friends of their parents, but the results were beginning to lead to 'outside' requests for her services. A good thing too, since she was going to have to turn down her agent's latest acting job offer.

'Hey, how come so serious?' Ryan asked, slipping up behind her and wrapping his arms around her waist. 'Worried your mum will discover the pavlova is store-bought?' he teased, nibbling her neck.

'Shh!' she hissed. 'She might hear, and I'm trying to impress her with domesticity and home entertaining skills.'

'Don't worry,' he murmured, with lips that skimmed her bare shoulders. 'Your "home entertaining" impresses the hell out of me. Want me to tell her what you can do in a hallway?'

She laughed. 'Don't you dare! I can just hear her now. "You made poor Ryan roll naked on the carpet when there was a perfectly good bed inside?"' Her body felt his quake with amusement. 'Gosh, it'd be worse than the time I put the milk carton on the table when Reverend Evans came to visit.'

'Worse than that, huh?' He turned her around and managed to send her weak-kneed with just one very thorough kiss.

'Much worse,' she agreed, clinging to him until she was sure she could stand. 'Mum likes you heaps more than she did Reverend Evans.'

'How about you? Do you like me better?'

'Yeah.' She grinned.

'Glad to hear it.'

'I've got something else you'll be glad to hear. I won't be doing that second condom commercial.'

Ryan felt guilty that he'd obviously come out the victor in what had been an ongoing disagreement between them since her agent had advised her about the commercial three weeks ago. While he couldn't deny that Kirrily would be donating her talents to a deserving campaign, the script for the proposed commercial was risqué enough to attract the interest of weirdos, and Ryan hated the thought of her being in that particular line of fire. Still, he felt like a heel.

'Look,' he said, tilting her chin, 'if you really want to do it…do it.'

Her delight was evident. 'You mean it won't bother you?'

'Hell, yes, it'll bother me! But you've got to do what *you* want to do, not what I want.' He sighed. 'It's entirely your decision.'

Her gypsy beauty was illuminated with a wide, self-satisfied smile. 'You look so *cute* when you're being noble,' she teased, drawing a finger along his lower lip. 'But the decision has been taken out of my hands by a higher power—although you're partly responsible.'

He groaned. 'I'm sorry, sweetheart,' he said, genuinely contrite. 'I guess the producer didn't appreciate me telling him the script stank?'

'Oh, that didn't bother him!' she dismissed. 'He told Carole he doubted you had a creative bone in your whole body.'

'Smart-alec—'

'No, what he didn't appreciate was the idea of having one of the stars of a safe sex infomercial pregnant—something about it lacking credibility...' Kirrily paused and waited. And waited and *waited*. '*Ry...an!*'

'You're *pregnant*! You're going to have a baby?'

She fought for a droll look. 'No, I'm pregnant and going to have a kitten! Of course—' She was hoisted into the air with a whoop of male joy so loud that they must have heard it in Sydney, but the pure unadulterated love shining in Ryan's face as he held her above his head spoke even louder. He lowered her back to the floor with infinite gentleness.

'When?' he asked.

'Mid-July. I...I found out yesterday, but I wanted it to be a New Year's present for you.'

'You'll never give me a better one, honey.' His voice was uneven and his hands trembled as they framed her face. 'I don't think it's possible to love anyone more than I love you this minute.'

'Mmm...me neither,' she whispered, unable to halt the tears of happiness slipping onto her cheeks. Ryan caught them with the tip of his tongue, then delivered a kiss so tender that it touched her soul. Ryan wasn't just the best thing in her life, he *was* her life.

'I love you so much, Kirrily Claire Talbot,' he said, when he lifted his head.

Hugging him tight, she smiled. 'Too bad we've got a yard full of guests or you could have shown me how much.' He blinked as if he'd only just remembered the fact, before a pride-filled grin split his face.

'C'mon,' he said, grasping her hand. 'We've got an announcement to make.'

Kirrily stalled just for a moment. 'I hope we have a boy and he turns out exactly like you.'

'Really? I'd kinda like a girl who's as smart, beautiful and...' He paused and shook his head. 'No, on second thoughts a boy like me *would* be best.' His grin was pure torment. '*One* female like you is more than even I can probably deal with in this lifetime!'

'Rat!' she retorted, laughing as she hurried after him. 'In that case, I think I'll have a girl just to spite you, Ryan Talbot!'

And seven months later she did just that!

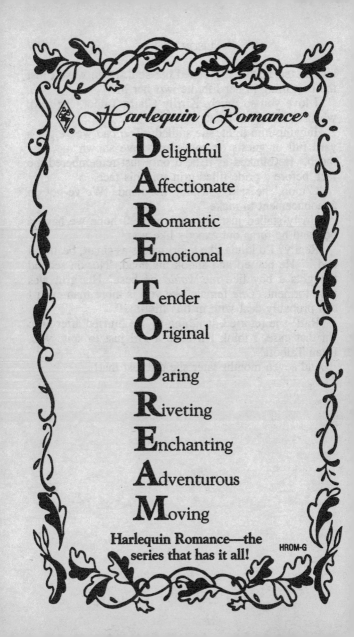

Harlequin Romance®

Delightful
Affectionate
Romantic
Emotional
Tender
Original
Daring
Riveting
Enchanting
Adventurous
Moving

Harlequin Romance—the
series that has it all!

HROM-G

Harlequin® Historical

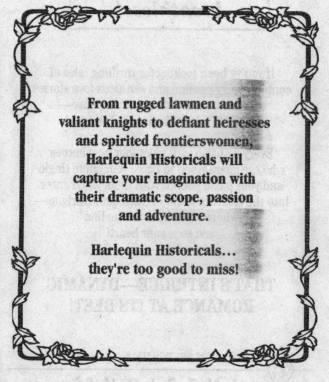

From rugged lawmen and
valiant knights to defiant heiresses
and spirited frontierswomen,
Harlequin Historicals will
capture your imagination with
their dramatic scope, passion
and adventure.

Harlequin Historicals...
they're too good to miss!

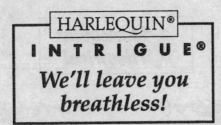

LOOK FOR OUR FOUR FABULOUS MEN!

Each month some of today's bestselling authors bring
four new fabulous men to Harlequin American Romance.
Whether they're rebel ranchers, millionaire power brokers
or sexy single dads, they're all gallant princes—and
they're all ready to sweep you into lighthearted fantasies
and contemporary fairy tales where anything is possible
and where all your dreams come true!

You don't even have to make a wish…
Harlequin American Romance will grant your every desire!

Look for Harlequin American Romance
wherever Harlequin books are sold!